Waiting for the Parade

WAITING FOR THE PARADE

a play by
John Murrell

Talonbooks • Vancouver • 1980

published with assistance from the Canada Council and
Alberta Culture.

Talonbooks
201 1019 East Cordova
Vancouver
British Columbia V6A 1M8
Canada

This book was typeset by Linda Gilbert, designed by
David Robinson and printed in Canada by Hignell Printing Limite

Second printing: August, 1984
Third printing: August, 1985
Fourth printing: May, 1986
Fifth printing: August, 1988

Rights to produce *Waiting for the Parade*, in whole or in part,
in any medium by any group, amateur or professional,
are retained by the author and interested persons are requested
to apply to his agent Susan Schulman, 165 West End Avenue,
New York, New York, U.S.A. 10023.

Canadian Cataloguing in Publication Data

    Murrell, John, 1945 -
      Waiting for the parade

    ISBN 0-88922-183-9

    I. Title.
    PS8576.U77W3   C812' .54   C81-091054-3
    PR9199.3.M87W3

Waiting for the Parade was first performed at Alberta Theatre Projects at the Canmore Opera House, Heritage Park, Calgary, Alberta on February 4, 1977, with the following cast:

Catherine	Sheila Moore
Janet	Marie Baron
Margaret	Joan Boyd
Eve	Patricia Connor
Marta	Merrilyn Gann

Directed by Douglas Riske
Designed by George Dexter
Costumes by Jane Grose
Lighting by Peter Van Johnson
Properties by Paul Joyal

Waiting for the Parade was also performed at the Lyric Theatre Hammersmith in London, England on November 20, 1979, with the following cast:

Catherine	Fiona Reid
Janet	Frances Cuka
Margaret	June Watson
Eve	Beth Morris
Marta	Deborah Norton

Directed by Richard Cottrell
Set and Costumes by Alix Stone
Lighting by John B. Reid

The author wishes to acknowledge with profound gratitude the talent and advice of the following actresses and directors, without whom *Waiting for the Parade* in finished form would simply not have been possible: Kathie Ball, Clare Coulter, Carole Galloway, Angela Gann, Nonnie Griffin, Kay Hawtrey, Susan Hogan, Rita Howell, Nancy Kerr, Patricia Ludwick, Mickey MacDonald, Judy Marshak, Joan Orenstein, Mary Trainor, Karen Wood, David Hemblen, Eric Steiner and Scott Swan.

THE CHARACTERS:

CATHERINE, *in her early thirties.*
JANET, *in her late thirties.*
MARGARET, *in her fifties.*
EVE, *in her twenties.*
MARTA, *in her thirties.*

Scene One

Darkness.

A rattle of drums is heard, exploding into a march, like a regiment of Canadian infantry about to hit the parade ground.

This continues for a few seconds, then fades into a swing tune, played in the Glenn Miller style, loud. The two pieces of music contend for a moment, then the swing tune swamps the march, which fades quickly. The swing tune continues.

The lights come up on five women, standing or seated, waiting.

JANET is standing, holding on to the back of a chair, moving her feet to the music, aggressively cheerful.

The others are motionless, moody or preoccupied. Pause. They wait.

Eventually JANET crosses to CATHERINE, taps her on the shoulder and nods towards the dance floor. CATHERINE shrugs and they move onto the dance floor together.

*They dance for a moment. Both know the latest steps. Then
JANET tramps on CATHERINE's toes. CATHERINE winces,
limps away to the edge of the stage where she sits, takes
off one of her toeless pumps, and massages her foot.*

Pause.

*JANET looks all around, then crosses to MARGARET,
taps her on the shoulder and nods towards the dance floor.
MARGARET grimaces, but allows JANET to drag her to
the perimeter of the dance floor. They dance. MARGARET
executes a few furtive, old-fashioned steps, awkwardly.
JANET tries to "spin" her. MARGARET stumbles. Angry
and embarrassed, she pushes JANET away, hastily returns
to her chair and sits, turning her back on the others.*

Pause.

*JANET looks all around. She crosses towards MARTA who is
sitting apart, her back also turned. As JANET approaches,
MARTA swivels around and looks at her. JANET recognizes
MARTA, stops, smiles very feebly, and quickly moves away
in the opposite direction. MARTA turns her back again.*

Pause.

*JANET sees EVE, crosses to her, taps her on the shoulder
and nods towards the dance floor. EVE hesitates but finally
accepts, unhappily. She and JANET move onto the dance
floor. They dance — JANET, anxious but determined,
smiling; EVE, nervous and growing unhappier by the moment
as she watches her feet. JANET's dancing becomes livelier.
She is literally propelling EVE around the dance floor.
EVE tries to break away from her, whispering incoherent
apologies. JANET pulls her back again and forces her to dance.*

*Suddenly EVE bursts into loud sobs, pulls free of JANET
roughly and covers her face with both hands. She crosses
upstage, takes out a handkerchief and blows her nose. She
continues sobbing, her body shaking.*

Pause.

JANET looks around, lost. Pause. She returns to her chair, stands behind it as before, fastens her hands to the back of it, begins moving her feet to the swing tune. She tries to smile.

The five women wait.

The swing tune comes to a rousing conclusion.

The lights fade to a glow on all except CATHERINE.

Scene Two

CATHERINE is alone. She speaks to the audience.

CATHERINE: My God, he was so proud of himself! One of the first to volunteer! Smiling like the halfwit boy who helped out on my uncle's farm at harvest time. "Canada's finest — on parade!" He saluted me. Clicked his heels. And kissed me. I could've knocked him flat! That night, when he crawled into bed beside me, I was still mad as hell. "You might've said something to me first," I told him. "You might've wondered if I can manage on my own. If I need a little time to work things out!" He just cuddled up closer. Kept right on grinning. Like the halfwit boy on my uncle's farm, who used to show off for the girls by dropping his pants.   *Pause.* He reached across and pulled my hair back from my face. "Jesus, you look like Ann Sheridan," he said. *Suggestively.*   "And you *know* how I feel about Ann Sheridan!"   *She laughs softly.*   It's not that I'm not proud of him. He looked like a million in his uniform. That terrible khaki didn't turn him into a ghost, like it does most of them. But somewhere inside a man's big skull, along with the honour and the glory — and the charm — there ought to be some space for good sense and — a little mutual respect. That's all I'm saying.

Scene Three

JANET, MARGARET, CATHERINE, EVE.

They gather around a Red Cross box which has long strips of sterile gauze inside it.

CATHERINE and MARGARET work as a team, rolling bandages of gauze, fastening them, putting them on a metal tray. JANET and EVE are another team.

JANET, in charge, occasionally "makes the rounds," inspecting the others' work.

JANET: *Tight.* Please remember. Nice and *tight.*

MARGARET: Nice and *tight.*   *To CATHERINE, as JANET moves away.*   I can't stand that woman.

CATHERINE: She's okay. She does her bit.

MARGARET: Oh yes. And then some.

JANET: Edges *straight.*

EVE: Edges *straight.*

MARGARET: Did you see those little turbans they have on sale, down at the Bay?

CATHERINE: I don't think so.

MARGARET: "Durbin turbans," they're called. For Deanna Durbin. With polka dots. They're all the rage. You should get down there and have a look. A turban would suit you.

JANET: Straighten but don't *stretch.*

EVE: Don't *stretch.*

MARGARET: I wish I could wear a hat. Nothing I'd love better. But I put on a hat, and my head turns into a balloon! Awful.

JANET: Nice and *tight*.

EVE: Nice and *tight*.

MARGARET: Did you get a letter this week?

CATHERINE: Not yet.

MARGARET: Uh-oh.

CATHERINE: It's only Wednesday.

MARGARET: My sister has a son in the R.A.F. Said he couldn't wait until Canada manages to grow wings of her own. And he writes to her three times a day. Can you imagine? Three times, every day.

CATHERINE: That's sweet.

MARGARET: I told her I think it's a shameful waste of paper.

JANET: Edges *straight*!

MARGARET: Edges *straight*! *Aside to CATHERINE.* I can't stand that woman.

CATHERINE: What about your own family? Did your boys —?

MARGARET: Oh, don't talk to me about them!

EVE: I went to see *Intermezzo* last night. For the fourth time. Harry refused to go with me. He hates Leslie Howard. "Too fussy and feminine," he says. I don't agree. English gentlemen are just — different. And I say it's all to their credit.

JANET: Work quickly but work *carefully*.

EVE: *Carefully*.

MARGARET: Death runs in my family. That's what worries me. Sudden, unexpected death. My dad was only thirty-four years old when he started to wind down like an old clock. Dead and buried within six months! My husband — I won't even mention him. He never took proper care of himself. And now my oldest boy — twenty-one years old — tells me he's going down to the Tecumseh to enlist. "Might as well," he says, "before they call me up. They'll be calling us all up, sooner or later."

EVE: Oh, I don't think so. Prime Minister King promised we'd never have conscription in this country. Never.

MARGARET: He's anemic. Or the closest thing to it. Maybe they won't take him. He inherited a blood condition from his father.

JANET: Straighten but don't *stretch*.

MARGARET: I guess I'll lose my seventeen year old too, the day he graduates. And I know in my heart I'll never see either of them on this earth again. Runs in my family.

JANET: Nice and *tight*.

EVE: Nice and *tight*.

CATHERINE: Billy says the rain really gets to you over there. He says he'd heard all those stories about winter in the Old Country, but he really knew he was in for it when he dropped his wedding band into that English muck, and it disappeared like a pebble down a well.

MARGARET: Oh Lord. But he got his ring back, eh?

CATHERINE: I think so.

MARGARET: You don't want your husband over there — on the loose — without a shiny reminder on his left hand.

CATHERINE: I trust Billy.

MARGARET: Trust? *She laughs, one short, sarcastic caw.* Trust is one thing. Two or three years out of the nest is something else. He's a man, isn't he?

CATHERINE: Maybe you're right.

MARGARET: I know I'm right. *Pause.* Your little girl must miss him though.

CATHERINE: Yes. She does.

They work silently for a moment. Suddenly JANET crosses to MARGARET.

JANET: Stop! Stop everything!

MARGARET: What now?

JANET: *indicating MARGARET's and CATHERINE's bandages* These edges aren't *straight!*

MARGARET: They look straight to me.

JANET: I don't mean to sound like a sergeant-major, but either we do it according to instructions, or it's not worth doing at all! *Unrolling bandages.* These two will have to be done over. *As MARGARET groans.* Concentrate on your work. This isn't a socal gathering. *Looking at CATHERINE.* There's a war on.

CATHERINE: So I heard.

JANET: *returning to work* Nice and *tight.*

MARGARET: Nice and *tight.* *Aside to CATHERINE.* I can't stand that woman.

EVE: Yesterday in the staff room I felt like screaming.
    The principal announced we might not open school until
    the middle of October next year. To allow the farm
    students to help out at home as long as possible. Old
    Mr. Herbert, with the garlic breath, nodded. "Yes," he
    said, "so many of our strapping farm boys already
    training for this great conflict. They won't be home
    again for years. And many of them in no condition to
    lend a hand when they do come home." I wanted to
    scream at him: "How do you know? This whole mess
    could be over in a few months!" Couldn't it? Don't you
    think so?

JANET: Edges *straight*.

EVE: I read an editorial in the Toronto paper. It said
    Hitler couldn't possibly last more than six months.

*Softly, very far away, a Richard Tauber record begins to
play.*

JANET: Straighten but don't *stretch*.

EVE: It said a man has to believe in what he's fighting
    for, to hold out against such odds. And nobody could
    possibly believe in what Hitler says he believes in!

MARGARET: "Deutschland über alles." Oh, the man's
    a maniac, no question about that. But he's a *clever*
    maniac. That's the way those people are. That's the way
    God made them.

JANET: *a pronouncement   God's* had nothing to do with
    Germany for the past fifty years! Anybody knows that.

MARGARET: *aside to CATHERINE*   I can't stand that
    woman.

JANET: Nice and *tight*.

MARGARET: *to CATHERINE*   You really ought to go
   down and take a peek at those turbans. A turban would
   suit you.

The Tauber record continues, swells, into the next scene.

Scene Four

TAUBER:
   ". . . und mein Glück nahmst du mit dir;
   Gib mir wieder, was du fandest,"
   Etc.

*MARTA is alone, sewing and smoking. She speaks with a
slight, but noticeable German accent.*

MARTA: *to the audience*   "Always do the delicate
   work by hand," my father says. "A Singer sewing
   machine has no finesse."

Pause. She inspects the garment she's working on.

MARTA: "A man's jacket should be like his character,"
   my father says, "comfortable. With a little 'give' in the
   fabric. Able to take some punishment without looking
   shabby."

Pause. The record concludes.

TAUBER:
   "Teile es mit mir!
   Ja! mit mir!"

MARTA: He was never, at any time, a member of the Nazi
   party! I don't care how much of that garbage they found
   in our basement! After my mother died, he went a little
   crazy, that's all. Don't most old men go a little crazy?
   He started sending away to Berlin for magazines and
   newspapers and — German nationalism? It might just as

15

easily have been seed catalogues — or stomach remedies! Any silly thing for him to take an interest in. To keep him happy. Oh yes, they told me he joined the Bund — the "Canadians for Hitler" — whatever you call it. They showed me his membership card. Hidden under the office blotter. And two or three silly letters he got from some Reichscounsellor or Reichsminister or Reichs-something. "We're only doing our duty," they said. *Pause. Angry.* We have been in this country since I was nine years old! We don't know any Nazis! *Pause.* Tomorrow I'll drive out to the camp where they put him. I want to take him some tobacco. They sell cigarettes out there, but not to my father's taste. "Canadian smokes!" my father says, and he spits. "It's like they fill the paper with sawdust from a dirty stable!" *Pause.* He was never — at any time — a member of the Nazi party.

Scene Five

JANET sits at an upright piano. She plays an elaborate arpeggio.

JANET: *to the audience* Remember this one? All the fellows love it. *She sings.*
"Underneath the lantern, by the barracks gate,
Darling, I remember the way you used to wait."

EVE joins her.

JANET AND EVE: *singing*
"'Twas there that you whispered tenderly
That you loved me, you'd always be
My Lily of the Lamplight,
My own Lily Marlene."

EVE speaks to the audience while JANET "vamps" on the piano.

EVE: I think I was accosted on the streetcar this morning.
I'm not certain it was the poor soldier's fault. I kept
telling him, "Don't stand so close, please. I'm a married
woman!" But he may have been hard of hearing. Or an
Australian.

JANET AND EVE: *singing*
"Time would come for roll call, time for us to part —"

MARGARET joins them.

JANET, EVE AND MARGARET: *singing*
"Darling, I'd caress you, and press you to my heart.
And there, 'neath the dusty lantern light,
I'd hold you tight. We'd kiss goodnight,
My Lily of the Lamplight,
My own Lily Marlene."

MARGARET speaks to the audience while JANET "vamps."

MARGARET: He bumped right into me. At his age. And
he held out this big dripping cherry ice cream cone. And
he winked at me. At his age! And he said, *"Wanta lick?"*
"I'm going to report this," I told him, "Who's your
commanding officer? *"I'm* the commanding officer,"
he said.

JANET, EVE AND MARGARET: *singing*
"Give me a rose to show how much you care;
Tied to the stem, a lock of golden hair."

CATHERINE joins them.

JANET, EVE, MARGARET AND
CATHERINE: *singing*
"Surely tomorrow you'll feel blue?
But then will come a love that's new
For my Lily of the Lamplight,
For you, Lily Marlene."

JANET "vamps."

CATHERINE: *to the audience*   My God, I'd rather
    have a dinner date with a cannibal than a fast fox trot
    with a rookie flyer. "You put your hand there once
    more," I told him, "and I'm going to bite it!" His face
    lit up. "Oh yes, ma'am — *please!*"

JANET arpeggios.

JANET: Put a little more smile in it, girls. For the boys
    with a shine on their boots! Two — three — four

JANET, EVE, MARGARET AND
CATHERINE: *in harmony*
    "Underneath the lantern, by the barracks gate,
    Darling, I remember the way you —"

*A few measures behind, MARTA begins singing the same
song, clear and strong.*

MARTA: *singing*
    "Vor der Kaserne, vor dem grossen Tor,
    Stand eine Laterne —"

*The others gradually stop and listen to MARTA, who remains
at a distance, singing unaccompanied.*

MARTA: *singing*   "— und steht sie noch davor."

JANET: Oh. How terrible.

She stops playing. MARTA continues.

MARTA: *singing*
    "So woll'n wir da uns wierderseh'n,
    Bei der Laterne woll'n wir steh'n,
    Wie einst, Lili Marlene —"

JANET: *overlapping the above*   It never occurred to
    me, this song used to be . . . one of theirs.

MARTA: *singing* "Wie einst, Lili Marlene!"
   She speaks to the audience. He came into the shop and
said he wanted to buy a new shirt. To celebrate. "I just
made sergeant," he said, "How about them apples?"
But it wasn't only a shirt he was shopping for. I could
see that. He patted me on the cheek. *Heartily.*
"It's a swell little place you got here. Mr. G.'s Apparel
for Gentlemen. Mr. G.'s your old man, eh? What's the
'G' stand for?" I told him: "Grauenholz." He pulled
back his hand, like he was burnt. "Oh. You're Jewish,
eh?" "No." "Oh Christ," he said, "it's the Boche, right
here on Centre Street!" *She sings.*
"Uns're beiden Schatten sah'n wie einer aus —"

*JANET arpeggios fiercely and leads the others in a reprise
of the English version, in harmony, as though trying to
drown MARTA out.*

JANET, EVE, MARGARET AND
CATHERINE: *singing*
   "Time would come for roll call, time for us to part —"

MARTA: *singing* "Dass wir so lieb uns hatten —"

JANET, EVE, MARGARET AND
CATHERINE: *singing*
   "Darling, I'd caress you, and press you —" *Etc.*

MARTA: *singing* "— sah man gleich daraus —" *Etc.*

*The German and English lyrics tangle together. The
phrases of the melody blend in a discord and fade, as
EVE, MARGARET, CATHERINE and MARTA disperse
variously, still singing. JANET remains, finishes the song
strongly in English.*

JANET: *singing*
   "My Lily of the Lamplight,
   My own Lily Marlene!"

Scene Six

JANET, alone, segues from "Lily Marlene" to "God Save the King" in one neat modulation. She plays a few bars, then stops. She stands and smiles, speaking to the audience as though addressing a small, informal gathering.

JANET: I shook hands with them. Yes, both of them.
That's when it really started for me. May 26, 1939.
Of course, war hadn't been declared yet — wouldn't
be declared for months. But some of us knew what was
coming. We knew the significance of a Royal Visit at such
a time. And it was when I shook hands with them that
I understood the supreme sacrifices that would be
demanded of each of us. The Queen even spoke to me.
She has the loveliest complexion. She said, "The
weather's very pleasant, isn't it?" I told her, "We always
have a splendid May and June in Alberta. And July."
And while I chatted with Her Majesty, I said to myself,
"Yes. Yes, we're still children of this great Empire.
Though thousands of miles of sea and land may divide
us. We have traditions and beliefs we'd be willing to die
for. Even here in Canada!" If I had a brother or a son,
I'd be proud to see him go! I'd sing and I'd cheer and
I'd wave from the platform as his train disappeared into
the night!   *Slight pause.*   My husband wanted to
go. Desperately. But he's part of an "essential service."
He reads the Texaco News Flashes, afternoons and
evenings. And let me tell you, the miracle of radio is
one thing that holds this country together today!
*Pause. She smiles, takes a slip of paper from her pocket
and reads it.*   "The next meeting of the Red Triangle
Hostesses will be held this Tuesday at four in Room 6
of the YWCA. Subjects to be discussed include 'Welcome
to Calgary' handkerchiefs for our newly-arrived New
Zealanders. Also, contrary to rumour, the scrap metal
collection will continue until further notice."
A big smile.   Thank you.

Scene Seven

CATHERINE is standing in front of EVE, with her back to the audience, brushing EVE's hair. Both wear large towels around their shoulders.

CATHERINE: Stop wiggling! Wait a second. There. Now you're gorgeous.

She steps away from EVE. Both have put "fashionable" white streaks through their hair.

CATHERINE: Now you're perfection.

She gives EVE a hand mirror. EVE looks at herself.

EVE: Oh no. Harry will kill me.

CATHERINE: I like it.

EVE: If *he* doesn't kill me, the superintendent of schools will.   *She lowers the mirror.*   What do you really think?

CATHERINE: I think we're both gorgeous.

EVE: *looking in the mirror again*   I look like a cross between Rita Hayworth and a skunk.

CATHERINE laughs and tries to take the mirror from her.

CATHERINE: You'll get used to it.

EVE hangs on to the mirror.

EVE: Harry will kill me.

CATHERINE: Put the mirror down.

EVE: *still looking in the mirror*   It just isn't the proper image for an educator. You don't know. Those Grade 10's can be vicious.

CATHERINE: Put the mirror down! Give yourself a minute to adjust.

EVE: Harry will kill me.

CATHERINE: For God's sake, put the mirror down!

She reaches for the mirror. EVE quickly puts it down in her lap.

CATHERINE: Let's talk about something else.

EVE: All right.   *Pause.*   What?

CATHERINE: I got a letter yesterday.

She takes the letter from her dress pocket.

EVE: So you said.

CATHERINE: The first one in weeks. It's his second winter over there —   *She reads from the letter.*
"So cold and damp, the birds are dying of rheumatism in mid-air and dropping to the ground, dead on arrival."

EVE: Not seriously?

CATHERINE: Billy's afraid his regiment's gone sour on the war.   *She reads from the letter.*   "Six months we've been sitting around in tents, not enough room to stand up in. We're ready as we'll ever be, but nobody's said a word about moving any Canadians to the front. Another month and we'll be soft again."

Pause.

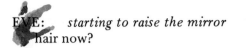EVE: *starting to raise the mirror* May I look at my hair now?

CATHERINE: Not yet.

EVE: *putting the mirror down* Well, do we have to talk about the war? I get enough of that from Harry. It'll only depress us. Isn't anything else happening in the world anymore?

CATHERINE: *putting the letter away* For instance?

Pause.

EVE: I was looking at our enrollment for next year. Guess how many boys have registered for Grade 12 Matric. Guess.

CATHERINE: I give up.

EVE: Eight. *Eight*. And half of those will be sneaking off to the recruiting station before mid-term. While I'm drilling them in the socio-political history of Greece, they're daydreaming about machine guns. "The Bren — the mighty Bren!" they call it.

She makes a loud noise, like a machine gun.

CATHERINE: Don't talk about the war. It'll only depress us.

EVE: Harry greets me with that insane noise at the breakfast table every morning. *She makes the machine gun noise again.* Then he laughs his head off. He's never fully recovered from being told he's too old for active service. *Pause.* I should've married someone nearer to my own age. Senility strikes early in Harry's family. *Pause. Raising the mirror again.* May I look at my hair now?

CATHERINE: Not yet!

She snatches the mirror, glances at her own hair, then lays the mirror aside.

EVE: Well, let's not talk about Harry anymore.

CATHERINE: I second that motion.

Pause.

EVE: Tell me about your work, down at the plant?

CATHERINE: Not much to tell. I make sandwiches. I sell Orange Kik and jujubes four times a day. It's somewhere to go, something to do. And I need the money.

EVE: Working around all those men — it doesn't make you nervous?

CATHERINE: Men have never made me nervous.

EVE: They've never made my anything but.   *Pause.* May I look at —?

CATHERINE: *Not yet.*

Pause.

EVE: Last week Harry joined the Mounted Constabulary.

CATHERINE: The what?

EVE: The Calgary Mounted Constabulary! Ta-ta! A bunch of old men with horses and chaps and pith helmets. From dusk to dawn they bravely patrol the Reservoir. On guard against enemy infiltration! I asked Harry, "Who would want to infiltrate a reservoir?" I thought he was going to hit me.   *Pause.*   Did you write Billy for permission to take a job?

CATHERINE: *laughs and shakes her head* He would've said "no."

EVE: And if he finds out, he'll be angry?

CATHERINE: He'll be ashamed. He'll feel like he's let us down.

EVE: But you don't feel that way?

CATHERINE: I try not to think about it. "There's a war on."

EVE: *rising suddenly* Please, please don't say that! I'm sick of hearing it! Listen, you know what the latest insanity is?

CATHERINE: Why don't you sit down?

EVE: *beginning to pace* I read that Leslie Howard has offered his services to the British war effort! *Leslie Howard!*

CATHERINE: Maybe you should look at your hair now.

EVE: I wanted to scream! And they're bombing Great Britain! *Great Britain!*

CATHERINE: I know that. Billy's there.

EVE: They're bombing Great Britain! They're bombing France! They're bombing Norway! They're bombing Belgium! We're back in the Dark Ages! Wasting lives, spilling blood all over Europe!

CATHERINE: Sit down!

EVE: *pacing more and more frantically*   And Leslie
    Howard's in the middle of all that! An actor! A
    distinguished artist! Your Billy can hardly wait for a
    chance to be part of the slaughter! And my husband
    would be leading the dance of death with a sabre if he
    weren't too old! But they said it'd all be over in a few
    months! I remember an editorial — in the Toronto
    paper —! Oh God!

*CATHERINE has risen, crosses to EVE, catches her by the
shoulders and shakes her. Pause. EVE's head droops.*

EVE: Sorry. The first thing they taught us at Normal
    School was self-control. An educator mustn't lose her
    grip on herself. Sorry.

CATHERINE: At least you forgot about your damned
    hair for a minute.   *Putting one arm around EVE's
    shoulders, she offers her the mirror.*   Go ahead. Take
    a peek. And I'll buy you a Coca Cola if you don't feel
    one hundred per cent better about it now.

*EVE takes the mirror, holds it close and looks at herself.
She bursts into tears, drops the mirror and covers her face
with both hands. CATHERINE holds her.*

Scene Eight

MARGARET, alone, gets to her knees, with some difficulty.

MARGARET: Our Father which art in Heaven. Hallowed
    be Thy name. Thy kingdom come. Thy will be done . . .
    I had to talk with someone tonight, Lord. Otherwise you
    know I won't get a wink of sleep. You understand. You
    understand everything.   *Pause.*   I went downtown
    this afternoon, to buy five pounds of sugar. For some
    fudge to send to my boy in Halifax. There was only one
    sack left on the shelf and a big fat woman grabbed it
    before I could. Something has to be done about the

hoarding situation in this city! Tonight I have a lot of hatred and rancor in my heart towards that woman, Lord. That fudge might've been the last thing I ever sent to my boy. He's on convoy service. You know what that means. Those U-boats! They sink more ships than they let slip through. Somewhere — deep in my heart — I know I'll never see him on this earth again. Runs in my family. *Pause.* In Jesus' name. Amen. *She starts to rise, then suddenly sinks to her knees again.* No. There's something else. My eighteen year old. He's never at home anymore. I can't imagine where he goes or what he does. I'm afraid to imagine. Last Sunday I asked him to go to church with me. He told me he doesn't believe in God the Father, God the Son, or any other gods. Well, I gave him such a swat! The older one went through the atheist stage too. You understand, Lord — he's not serious about it. *Pause.* It can't be dances that he goes to. He doesn't believe in those either. *Pause.* I'm tired. I'll have to leave this one with you a while, Lord. Maybe we can work on it together? *Suddenly she winces, inhales sharply, grabs her side as though in pain, massages it for a moment, then relaxes a bit.* It's — it's nothing. I'm tired. That's all. Tired. Who isn't? *Pause.* In Jesus' name. *Pause.* I don't know what I'd do without Him. *Pause.* Amen.

She stands, wincing again slightly.

MARGARET: I should finish putting those pickles away. Who'll eat them though? Nobody at home anymore. I could give some to the Sally Ann —

Scene Nine

The Richard Tauber record is heard, softly at first, then swelling.

TAUBER:
"Banger Gram, eh' sie kam,
Hat die Zukunft mir umhüllt,
Doch mit ihr blühte mir
Neues Dasein lusterfüllt,"
Etc.

JANET is waiting impatiently, tapping her foot. After a moment, MARTA enters, smoking. She carries a pair of men's trousers, with chalk alteration marks, on a wooden hanger.

The Tauber record continues in the background, rather loud.

JANET: Good afternoon. I rang the bell on the counter, but nobody came.

MARTA: Sometimes I don't hear the bell.

JANET: No? I'm not surprised.

Pause.

MARTA: Can I show you something?

JANET: No.

MARTA: Just browsing?

JANET: No. I didn't come in to buy anything.

MARTA: Oh?

Pause.

JANET: Look, I'll come straight to the point — if I may?

MARTA: What point?

JANET: We felt it was necessary — at least, I did — I thought you and I should — have a little chat.

MARTA: I see.   *Pause.*   Go on then. Chat.

JANET: It's about — about this music of yours.

MARTA: Music?

JANET: On the phonograph.

MARTA: Oh. You don't like it?

JANET: The question is not whether *I* like it —

MARTA: No? What is the question then?

Pause.

JANET: *softly*   You're not making this any easier. People — a substantial number of people — are bothered by it.

MARTA: By my music?

JANET: Yes.

MARTA: Why?

JANET: Surely I don't have to tell you — Would you mind putting out your cigarette?

MARTA: Yes, I would. Who is it that objects to my music?

JANET: As a matter of fact, I was delegated — unoffically — A substantial number of people have expressed their disapproval. Concern. And I feel it's in your own best interest —

MARTA: Because it's German music, you mean?

JANET: Surely you can understand that.

MARTA: It's not war music. It's a love song.

JANET: I realize that. I am a music lover myself —

MARTA: Are you? Don't you like this song?

JANET: It's — a lovely melody.

MARTA: You want me to translate the words? "Ach, so fromm" — "Oh, so chaste" — "Ach, so traut" — "Oh, so true" —

JANET: Please! You're not making this any easier. There are constant complaints about that noise! That music. It can be heard right out there on Centre Street. You must know that.

MARTA: These old buildings have very thin walls. I wish I could afford a better place. I just like to have some music while I work —

JANET: The point is, nobody wants to hear it!

MARTA: *I* want to hear it!

She lights another cigarette.

JANET: Look, I came here with every intention of being perfectly pleasant.

MARTA: Oh, you *are* being "perfectly pleasant."

JANET: I can understand that you might feel a bit —
    resentful. I know all about your father. Where he is.
    And why. You have my sympathy. Truly. But it's in your
    own best interest to be a little more — discreet. When
    they asked me to come here, I told them, "I'm sure
    she's not a real die-hard like her father. She's been in
    this country quite a few years now —"

MARTA: Since I was nine years old!

JANET: Don't raise your voice to me! I'm trying to make
    this as painless as possible. For your sake!

The Tauber record concludes.

TAUBER:
    "Teile es mit mir!
    Ja! mit mir!"

MARTA: Get out of my shop.

JANET: Civic authorities can be asked to handle this sort
    of thing. But I thought —

MARTA: Get out of my shop.

JANET: — that you'd prefer a more personal approach.
    Obviously I was —

MARTA: *Get out of my shop.*

*JANET, totally frustrated, starts to leave, stops, turns back,
crosses swiftly to MARTA, grabs the trousers from her, rips
them off the hanger, throws the hanger down, violently
rumples the trousers and throws them down also, then exits
quickly. Pause. MARTA laughs without smiling and stoops
to pick up the trousers.*

MARTA: *singing to herself*
   "Banger Gram, eh' sie kam,
   Hat die Zukunft mir umhüllt,
   Doch mit ihr blühte mir
   Neues Dasein —"
   Etc.

The "Beer Barrel Polka," sung by a men's chorus, begins far away, growing nearer, swelling. It drowns out MARTA's voice and continues into the following scene.

Scene Ten

The polka crescendos and continues for a full chorus. On top of this, fade up the sounds of a troop train, departing the station — wheels squealing, steam, men's shouted goodbyes.

EVE, JANET and MARGARET are at the edge of the stage, waving energetically to the departing train.

There is a long table with fruit, knitted socks, miniature Union Jacks, etc. strewn over it. Underneath the table is a large cardboard box.

After a while the polka fades, followed a few moments later by the train sounds.

The three women stop waving, relax. JANET and MARGARET cross to the long table, begin rearranging the "hand-outs" on it, and stoop to rummage for fresh supplies in the box underneath.

EVE paces, stretching her legs. She speaks to the audience.

EVE: When Harry knows I've been down here — spreading
        cheer and knitted woolens among the men on their way
        East — he always meets me at the door, grinning like a
        bridegroom. "How were our boys looking? How were
        they feeling? Did you tell 'em to give the Führer hell
        for me? What's the latest scuttlebutt down there?"
        Scuttlebutt!

*CATHERINE rushes in, waves hello and joins the two women
at the table.*

JANET: Where were you?

CATHERINE: I missed the last streetcar from the plant.

JANET: We could all find excuses. We've had two
        trainloads through here already.

CATHERINE: It won't happen again.

EVE: *speaking to the audience*   I told Harry, "All I
        see down there are a lot of terrified, smiling young men.
        Desperate for a soft word and the smell of something
        feminine."

JANET: *shouting to EVE*   Did you come down here
        to work or just to moon around as usual?

EVE: Sorry.

*EVE joins the others at the table. They work silently for a
moment. Suddenly JANET shoves the others away, digs
right to the bottom of the cardboard box, then looks up,
in disbelief.*

JANET: Pears! *Pears.* Don't we have any more pears?
        She digs again for a moment, then looks up.   We
        actually don't have any more pears?

EVE: None on the table.

JANET: I can see that.

MARGARET: In the box?

JANET: No.

MARGARET: Then I guess we don't have any more
    pears.

JANET: Apples, oranges, small clusters of grapes, and
    pears. Isn't that what we agreed on?   *Wearily.*
    Who is responsible for pears?

CATHERINE: *wearily*   I am.

JANET: Then why don't we have any? It's just not as
    attractive without that touch of green. We have red,
    orange and purple. No green. Not nearly as attractive.

CATHERINE: I meant to buy pears this morning, but
    I — I didn't. I'm not feeling very well.

JANET: Don't tell me you're sick.

CATHERINE: Just tired. We've been working double
    shifts at the plant this week. I must've made fifty million
    tuna sandwiches.

JANET: Well, you can't get sick tonight. I don't have
    anybody to fill in for you.

EVE: I can fill in for her.

JANET: Absolutely not. That'd leave only three of us.
    Our energy level would go down. The boys would notice.
    They have every right to find us cheerful and full of vim.
    That takes at least four of us.

CATHERINE: I'm not sick! I'm tired.

JANET: Well, we won't be able to get any pears tonight. It's just not the same without something green. Any suggestions?

Slight pause.

MARGARET: I could run home and bring back some pickles.

JANET: I am trying to be serious about this.

MARGARET: Why not? Two or three big dills wrapped up in cellophane. They're using that lovely cellophane for everything now.

EVE: Somehow pickles don't seem very cheerful.

MARGARET: You haven't tasted *my* pickles.

JANET: *a pronouncement*   Pickles are out.

Pause.

EVE: Have we considered seedless grapes?

JANET: We're already giving them grapes.

EVE: Not green grapes.

JANET: I am trying to be serious about this!

Pause.

CATHERINE: Why don't we just hand out some of the sewing kits, those bachelor sewing kits we made up?

JANET: Didn't we agree those would be given only on request? It's not every man that knows his way around a needle and thread.

MARGARET: *to CATHERINE, but aimed at JANET*
Besides, they're not *green*.

Pause.

CATHERINE: *as JANET continues to ponder*   Oh for
God's sake, another trainload of boys may arrive any
minute, and here we stand, fretting over our colour
scheme!

JANET glares at her — pause — then sighs profoundly.

JANET: All right then. A few sewing kits at that end of
the table. It's better than nothing, I guess. Next time
it's our turn down here, it would be nice to have some
pears. As pre-arranged. Let's get busy.

*They go back to work, replenishing the table with fruit,
socks, Union Jacks, etc. JANET passes around the bachelor
sewing kits.*

JANET: And please check to ensure there are two needles
in each kit. Somebody got a little careless when they
were being assembled.   *She looks at EVE.*   No sense
doing it unless we do it right, is there?

They work.

CATHERINE: *to MARGARET*   Did you get a letter
this week?

MARGARET: *nods*   They transferred my boy to a
"corvette." I thought that was some kind of fish.

CATHERINE: Pass me some grapes.

MARGARET: The North Atlantic, you know. Lost to me
forever. No sense even hoping he'll ever come home
again.

CATHERINE: I haven't heard from Billy for nearly a month. Something must finally be happening over there.

MARGARET: And my younger one! I cornered him outside the bathroom this morning. "If you don't believe in this war," I told him, "you could at least get a job and help out with the rent. They'll be calling you up one of these days, whether you believe in it or not!"

EVE: Oh no. The Prime Minister promised he'd never resort to conscription.

JANET: And let's all try to remember the value of a smile. *To EVE.* I was watching you with that last bunch. You looked like you were in pain. These boys don't want to see that.

EVE: Sorry.

JANET: Remember, too much sentiment is worse than none at all.

EVE: I can't help it! When I think about where they're going, what they'll face there —!

JANET: Don't think about that! Tell them how swell they look. Tell them they're fighting to preserve a way of life that's precious to you. Think about them, not yourself —

CATHERINE: Oh, leave her alone!

MARGARET: Yes, for heaven's sake —

JANET: Let me remind you, I'm in charge here! I'm *responsible*!

The others turn away from her. Pause.

JANET: *quietly* And I'm perfectly aware what you
think of me. All of you. But I'm not concerned about
that now. I told my husband, "What does it matter
what they think about us, about either of us — as long
as we know we're contributing all we can?" *Pause.*
I wouldn't have volunteered to organize things down
here if I wanted to be Miss Popularity. *Pause.*
And those Texaco News Flashes hold this country
together. They do! *Pause.* I only hope, some day,
you will all realize that someone must be responsible —
in times like these — *She is near tears.* It isn't *us*
that matters — is it? —

The whistle of an approaching train, in the distance, is heard.

JANET: *pulling herself together* Here they are! Are we
all ready?

CATHERINE: I think so.

*There is a very slow crescendo of train noises to the end of
the scene.*

JANET: And let's remember: it's no time to be bashful.
If they don't start the ball rolling, you make the first
move. Some of these boys've never been away from home
before. You can talk to them about Pearl Harbour, about
the Yankees getting into the war. That's the latest
scuttlebutt.

EVE: *Scuttlebutt!*

MARGARET: *aside to CATHERINE* I can't stand
that woman.

*JANET has taken a pitch pipe from her pocket. The four
women move closer together. They are at the edge of the
stage, facing off in the direction from which the train is
approaching. JANET sniffles one last time, and then blows
on the pitch pipe.*

ALL FOUR: *led by JANET, they sing in harmony,*
    with bits of solo work
    "There'll be bluebirds over
    The white cliffs of Dover
    Tomorrow, just you wait and see.

    There'll be love and laughter
    And peace ever after
    Tomorrow, when the world is free.

    The shepherd will tend his sheep,
    The valley will bloom again,
    And Jimmy will go to sleep
    In his own little room again.

    There'll be bluebirds over,"
    Etc.

They continue singing as the train comes into the station.
Sounds of squealing wheels, steam and men's shouted hellos
drown out the women's voices completely.

Scene Eleven

MARTA, wearing a coat and hat, carrying a purse, comes in,
sits on a chair and speaks to the audience as though to another
individual.

MARTA: Excuse me, I know how busy you are, I won't
    take much time . . . I would like to know why my father
    is being moved again . . . Grauenholz. Robert Grauenholz. . . .
    He wrote to me to say they're moving him again. To a
    camp farther south, more than a hundred miles away. . . .
    That's right. But why? . . . I have no idea. . . . No,
    I can't imagine unless — Well, it seems they've been
    keeping some soldiers out there lately — captured
    German soldiers — foreign soldiers — and my father's
    been giving them tobacco. . . . That's what they told me.
    Lending them tobacco. Does that automatically make

him a master spy? I swear to you, he never had a secret
radio transmitter in the basement or a private arsenal
buried in the backyard! . . . Yes, I know, it's not funny.
Angry.   You think it's funny to me? I have been in
this country since I was nine years old! I have friends
in this war — on our side! I read the casualty lists like
everybody else! I am a Canadian citizen!   *Pause.*
No. . . . No, he never applied for his papers, not as far
as I know. Nor my mother. . . . I'm not sure. . . . I don't
know. Maybe because they couldn't read or write English
so well. Maybe because he wanted to go back there to
die?   *Angry.*   Maybe because they were too fond of
beer and blood sausages?! . . . . I'm — I'm sorry. . . .
I know, you're only doing your duty. But I won't be able
to visit him very often if he's moved so far. I might not
be able to visit him at all. . . . Yes, I have a car, but it's
not a very good one. And now they're saying gasoline
will be harder to — I'm simply asking you to leave him
where he is. I'm not asking you to release him. I wouldn't
dream of asking for that! For him to be treated like a
human being! What would be the use?!   *Pause. She
quickly brings herself under control.*   I'm sorry. . . .
Yes, I know. I know it takes time. Everything takes
time. . . . Well, shall I wait then? . . . No, no, I'll wait,
I don't mind waiting. . . . What? . . . He's fifty-seven —
no, fifty-eight years old. . . . Yes. Thank you. I'll wait.

Long pause. She waits.

MARTA: *to herself*   I'll wait. . . .

Scene Twelve

*CATHERINE and EVE, in their slips, are painting their legs.
MARGARET watches them.*

MARGARET: Well, it might fool some poor Aussie
   who knows more about sheep than about women. It
   certainly wouldn't fool me.

CATHERINE: It has to dry first.

MARGARET: Wet or dry, it wouldn't fool me.

CATHERINE: Everyone's using it. You can't tell it from the real thing.

EVE: Harry gives me money for the genuine article, silk. But when he told me how much he despises "those women who put paint on their limbs" — "tramps" he calls them — I knew I had to try it!

She and CATHERINE laugh.

MARGARET: When he finds out, he's going to kill you.

EVE: He won't find out. Harry would be the last to notice.

MARGARET: Oh? It's like that.

EVE: Like what?

CATHERINE: Careful. You're getting it all over your slip.

EVE: I really like it. I do. We're going to be gorgeous.

CATHERINE: You know what the guys down at the plant say: "You ain't seen nothin' yet!" We still have to put on our seams.

EVE: Seams?

CATHERINE brandishes an eyebrow pencil. She and EVE laugh.

CATHERINE: *to EVE*   Excuse me, I believe your left "limb" is just about ready.

EVE: You're going to do it, aren't you? I'm a little shaky.

CATHERINE: Hold still now.

She draws a "seam" on EVE's leg with the eyebrow pencil.

CATHERINE: Hold still!

MARGARET: *looking on*   Seams? That wouldn't fool me, not for a minute.

CATHERINE: *finishing the "seam"*   There! Now you do me. My right side's dry.

EVE: I'm not sure I —

CATHERINE: Sure you can. Just take it nice and slow.

EVE draws on CATHERINE's "seam."

CATHERINE: Oh — my God, you'll have to bear down harder! I'm ticklish!

EVE: I read somewhere that ticklish women are more aware of the potential of their bodies.

She and CATHERINE laugh.

EVE: I did. I read that in the *Home Companion*.

MARGARET: Okay. Let's drag our minds out of the gutter.

CATHERINE: Cheese it! The parson's wife!

She and EVE laugh. EVE stands back to examine CATHERINE's "seam."

EVE: How's that?

CATHERINE: How does it look?

MARGARET: Like somebody drew a line on your leg with an eyebrow pencil.

CATHERINE: My God, you're feeling jolly tonight.

MARGARET: However I feel, I have a right to feel that way.

CATHERINE: Why don't you go home if you're determined to be a wet blanket?

MARGARET: Don't talk to me like that!

EVE: Please, girls —

MARGARET: You don't know how I feel, or why!

CATHERINE: But I bet, if I wait a few seconds, I'm going to find out!

EVE: *quickly to CATHERINE* You want to do my other side now?

CATHERINE: Sure. All right.

CATHERINE starts to draw EVE's other "seam."

MARGARET: You two think you have troubles? You don't know what trouble is.

EVE: We *all* know what trouble is.

MARGARET: No! *You don't know!*

CATHERINE: What's wrong with you?!

Pause.

MARGARET: My son was arrested this morning.

CATHERINE: What?

EVE: The military police?

MARGARET: Not him. My other son.

CATHERINE: Arrested? For what?

EVE: Why didn't you say something before?

MARGARET: *turning away from them*   I'm just so . . .
ashamed. Humiliated.

Pause.

EVE: A lot of boys have been arrested for enlisting, then
backing out at the last minute. Not showing up for —

MARGARET: It's not that! I wish it was.

CATHERINE: Are you going to tell us or not?

MARGARET: They picked him up at the Stampede
grounds, down by the river —

CATHERINE: For what?

MARGARET: He was passing out pamphlets.

EVE: Pamphlets?

MARGARET: That's right. For the Communists!

CATHERINE: What are you talking about?

MARGARET: Yes, Communist anti-war propaganda!
I never heard of that before. The Russians are
Communists, and I thought they were on our side.
Aren't the Russians on our side?

EVE: I don't think anybody's very sure about the
Russians.

MARGARET: They threw him in jail! He'll have to stand trial, it'll be in the newspaper! Oh, I wish I were dead!

EVE: Don't say that.

CATHERINE: He's in jail now?

MARGARET: *nodding* They haven't posted bail. The constable told me they may not post it at all. Because this is a — federal offense — sedition or something.

She is weeping.

CATHERINE: My God.

MARGARET: I went down to see him this afternoon, as soon as I was notified. But they say he doesn't want to see me. He told them he doesn't believe in family loyalties, something like that. They must think he's a mental case!

CATHERINE: My God.

MARGARET: He's not even nineteen. *Pause.* I can't ever show my face again! *Pause.* What was he thinking about, pulling a stunt like that? Anti-war propaganda! There's not a judge or jury in the country that'd have mercy on him. I wouldn't have mercy on him if I were on the jury, I can tell you! *Pause.* And, oh Lord, they're cruel — they're brutal — up at Fort Saskatchewan, at the penitentiary. I read about it. They're uglier up there than the army or navy ever thought about being. Especially with a boy who —! *What was he thinking about?!* *Pause.* They'll kill him up there. That's both my sons. Gone. I'll never see either of them on this earth again.

Pause.

EVE: I think what he did is just as brave as what his brother's doing. In a different way. Don't you?

MARGARET: I don't know anything about that. I only know he hasn't one hope. And I'm all by myself now. Three months behind in the rent! That's all I know.

Long pause, then CATHERINE wets the end of the eyebrow pencil with her tongue and bends over awkwardly to finish her "seams."

EVE: *seeing her*   How can you do that — now?

CATHERINE: I have to do it. We promised we'd be in Bowness in half an hour, to instruct the boys from the wireless school in the two-step. Look, you missed a spot on your right leg. No, higher up. That's it.

Scene Thirteen

JANET sits alone, at the upright. She plays the rousing coda of a popular wartime song, then stands, smiles and speaks to the audience, as though to a large gathering.

JANET: No sense waiting for Neighbour Bill to set the example. You take the initiative and you'll be amazed how heartily others will follow your lead! Why, even at mealtime you can play your part in the defense of freedom. How? Does your family grumble and grouch about meatless days, the way mine does? Next time, surprise them with these attractive and tasty "Vegetable Sandwiches!"

She takes a large poster-board chart from the piano and holds it up. In bright colours the chart demonstrates the recipe she describes.

JANET: Take one half cup each of shredded carrot, shredded cabbage and shredded celery. Add three tablespoons of chopped watercress. You may substitute parsley. Moisten with a little mayonnaise, season with salt and pepper. Maybe a dash of Worcestershire sauce? And spread onto buttered slices of white or whole wheat bread. Cut diagonally and top with a thin slice of wholesome Canadian cheese. Umm-ummm! And don't forget, on days which aren't meatless, to save all your fat, bacon drippings and large bones. We need every spoonful of fat and every bone from every kitchen in this country! Fats make glycerine, you know, and glycerine is a major ingredient in many of our high explosives. There is enough hidden explosive power in ten pounds of fat to fire forty-nine anti-aircraft shells! *She pauses, for effect, then lays the chart aside.* And — to conclude —   *She folds her hands and recites earnestly:*

"However sharp your sorrow,
However harsh your plight,
The coming dawn will drive away
The terrors of your night.

However dark the stormclouds,
However deep your woes,
The watchword of the coming dawn is:
'Canadians, on your toes!!' "

On the last line, she elevates herself onto her tiptoes, making a "V For Victory" sign at the same time.

Obviously she imagines her recitation receiving a thunderous ovation. She bows, then bows again, and again, beaming proudly.

EVE enters upstage. JANET does not see her. She continues her bows. Becoming aware of EVE's presence, JANET wheels around.

JANET: *angry and embarrassed*   Where were you?!

EVE: Sorry, I —

JANET: Never mind. Let's get started.   *She sits at the piano.*   No sense doing it unless we're going to do it right, is there?

She plays a brief introduction, then the two women sing.

JANET AND EVE: *singing*
"Wish me luck as you wave me goodbye!
Cheerio, here I go, on my way!
Wish me luck as you wave me goodbye!
With a cheer, not a tear, make it gay!

Give me a smile I can keep all the while
In my heart while I'm away!

Till we meet once again, you and I,
Wish me luck as you wave me goodbye!

Big finish.

Wish me luck as you wave me goodbye!!"

JANET finishes with a flourish, then turns to EVE, who looks away, disappointed in her own performance.

JANET: A little better. That C sharp's still flat. And where's the *spirit*? We're not going to sell any bonds tomorrow with you looking like Garbo in *Camille*!

EVE: Sorry.

JANET: What's the problem here? Just keep telling yourself, we're going out onto that stage right after Walter Pidgeon! *Walter Pidgeon!*

EVE: I don't like Walter Pidgeon.

JANET: I am trying to be serious about this.

EVE: Sorry. Can we try it again?

JANET: I think we should. And where's the sunshine?

EVE smiles feebly.

JANET: Where's the *sunshine*?

EVE forces a larger, though not happier, smile.

JANET: A little better. With the gestures this time.

EVE: Oh, not the gestures!

JANET: *With the gestures this time.*

She thumps out the introduction again.

JANET: One — two — and? —

She and EVE sing. EVE half-heartedly performs a set of stylized gestures, in the Andrews Sisters manner, interpreting the lyrics.

JANET AND EVE: *singing*
"Wish me luck as you wave me goodbye!"

JANET: Breathe!

JANET AND EVE: *singing*
"Cheerio, here I go, on my way!"

JANET: Breathe!

JANET AND EVE: *singing*
"Wish me luck as you wave me goodbye!
With a cheer, not a tear, make it gay!"
Etc.

*They continue as MARGARET enters upstage, unseen by
JANET, crosses to EVE and whispers something in her ear.
EVE whispers back, trying not to lose her place in the song.*

JANET: *without looking around, she shouts*   Sing up!

*MARGARET whispers something more to EVE. EVE is
visibly upset by what she hears. She glances at JANET who is
really getting into the number now, singing to the audience.*

*MARGARET and EVE sneak out upstage. JANET doesn't
notice. She finishes the song alone, very loud, with much
"sunshine." She turns to speak to EVE at the conclusion.
She looks all around and realizes she's been deserted. Furious,
she slams the piano lid, as the lights come up on the
following scene.*

Scene Fourteen

*CATHERINE and MARTA are laughing, smoking and
drinking.*

*After a moment, MARGARET and EVE join them.
They embrace CATHERINE.*

CATHERINE: Come in, come in! Join the festivities!
    "Let our mirth be unparalleled!" Some idiot in my
    high school class used to shout that at every party:
    "Let our mirth be unparalleled!"

EVE: We came as soon as we could.

MARGARET: As soon as we heard. You poor thing.

*CATHERINE hoists a large mason jar full of semi-
transparent liquor.*

CATHERINE: "Let our mirth be unparalleled!"

She and MARTA laugh.

EVE: *about the liquor*   What is that?

CATHERINE: Wait, here's a glass. It might even be clean.

She pours EVE a glass of the liquor. EVE sips it and makes a face.

EVE: *breathless*   That's — nice.

MARGARET: *indicating MARTA*   What's she doing here?

CATHERINE: Some boys threw a smoke bomb under her porch. So I invited her to stay with me until it — evaporates, or whatever smoke bombs do.

MARGARET: *slightly sotto voce*   Well, she's the last person I expected to see in this house — tonight!

CATHERINE: "Let our mirth be —!"   *To MARGARET.*   See if you can find another glass. Must be one somewhere . . .

She wanders away, looking for a glass, forgets what she's doing and wanders back.

MARGARET: *to EVE*   What is that stuff?

EVE holds out her glass. MARGARET sniffs it and backs away.

MARGARET: No wonder she's falling down.   *Calling to CATHERINE.*   Coffee will do for me. Just plain coffee. Do you have any coffee?

CATHERINE: Oh, don't drink coffee! It'll ruin your nerves.

MARGARET: Those were ruined years ago.

MARTA: *looking at the others through her glass*
I didn't think I was going to like it at first. But you
know, it tastes better all the time.

CATHERINE: *putting her arm around MARGARET*
Don't you want to try it? "You must try *everything*
at least once, or life's not worth the doctor's bills!"
Somebody down at the plant told me that. It's brewed
in a galvanized washtub. And I didn't have to stand in
line with a handful of ration coupons to get it. It's called
"War Widow's Weakness!"

She and MARTA laugh.

MARGARET: *pulling away*   This is terrible.

EVE: *to CATHERINE*   There aren't any war widows
here.

CATHERINE: Oh hell, *everybody's* a war widow.
Everybody I know.   *Slight pause.*   Why don't we
sing something? Somebody start a song!

Pause.

EVE: *singing, not very enthusiastically*
"There'll be bluebirds over
The white —"

CATHERINE: No, no! Not that! My God, you'll put us
all to bed with the blues! Doesn't anybody know —?
Listen. You all know this one!   *She sings:*
"What makes a lady of eighty go out on the loose?
Why does a gander meander in search of a goose?"

MARGARET: *overlapping*   I never liked that song.

CATHERINE: *ignoring her*
"What puts the kick in a chicken, the magic in June?"

MARTA joins in.

CATHERINE AND MARTA: *singing*
"It's just Elmer's Tune!"

MARGARET: *as they continue, overlapping*   I never
thought a song has to be smutty to be fun!

CATHERINE AND MARTA: *singing*
"The hurdy-gurdies, the birdies, the cop on the beat,
The candy-maker, the baker, the man on the street,
The city charmer, the farmer —"

MARGARET: *shouting them down*   I said, I don't like
that song!

They stop singing.

MARGARET: And it certainly doesn't seem very — very
appropriate — especially tonight.

Pause. CATHERINE moves very close to her, staggering a bit.

CATHERINE: How old *are* you anyway?

MARGARET: I beg your pardon!

CATHERINE: I always wanted to ask.

EVE: *singing, hopefully*
"The hurdy-gurdies, the birdies —"

CATHERINE: No! Shut up! We'll get back to Elmer in
a second.   *To MARGARET.*   Well?

MARGARET: How old do you think I am?

CATHERINE: I don't know. Not as old as you act, I
hope!

MARGARET: Listen here! —

CATHERINE: My God, *nobody's* that old — I hope!

MARGARET: I don't have to listen to this!

She starts out. EVE stops her.

EVE: *quietly*   Please! She's not herself.

MARGARET: *likewise*   I don't care who she is!

EVE: Think of all she's been through today!

MARGARET: That's no excuse for —

CATHERINE: *singing loudly*   "Listen! Listen —"

MARTA joins in again, in harmony.

CATHERINE AND MARTA: *singing*
  "There's a lot you're liable to be missin'!"

MARTA: *continuing alone*   "Singin', swingin' —"

CATHERINE: *to MARTA*   Wait a second! Your glass
  is empty! How did that happen?

*They laugh, then resume singing as CATHERINE refills
MARTA's glass.*

CATHERINE AND MARTA: *singing*
  "Any old way and any old time!
  The hurdy-gurdies, the birdies, the cop on the beat,
  The candy-maker, the baker —"

*CATHERINE fades out, takes a large drink. MARTA fades
a moment later.*

CATHERINE: It was — very peculiar. The boy came to
  the door this afternoon. I knew who he was, of course.
  And he said, "Are you all alone here, ma'am?" "Sure,"
  I said, "I'm all alone here. Most of the time." And he
  handed me the telegram anyway! I mean, why'd he
  bother to ask if I'm all alone, if he's going to hand me

the damned telegram anyway?! Isn't the whole idea that a woman's supposed to be with a friend or — a relative or somebody — when she receives the — Besides, I didn't think they gave a damn whether you were alone or not, unless it's a death message. Isn't that right?

EVE: That's right.

CATHERINE: *slowly, carefully*   I was expecting — the worst. I was actually — relieved — to learn that Billy is only — *only* missing!   *She laughs without smiling.* I think that telegraph boy was a little bit — wacky.

MARTA giggles.

MARGARET: Isn't there any coffee? I'm not the only one who could use some.

MARTA: *offering her glass*   Don't you want a little sip of this?

MARGARET: I'm not talking to you!

MARTA smiles. Pause.

CATHERINE: Then, about half an hour later, a very nervous personnel officer phoned from downtown. To ask if I'd received the "unfortunate news."

EVE: Oh no!

CATHERINE: *laughs*   I think this war's made them all a little bit — wacky. What would that nervous personnel officer have done if I'd said: "My God, no! *What* unfortunate news?" I might've become hysterical or had fits or something. I mean, some women become hysterical, don't they?

EVE: I would have.

Pause. CATHERINE fills her own glass again and drinks.

EVE: But there's really no reason to get hysterical. Yet. Is there? In the first War, Harry's brother was missing in action for two years. When it was all over, they found him in a little town in Austria. The enemy had given him a job as a desk clerk in a sort of military hotel. And he didn't know one word of the language when he went over there. *She looks at MARTA and smiles feebly.* He was never even a prisoner, not really. Just a hotel clerk. Harry told me . . . *Realizing no one is listening to her, she fades out gradually.* It's the only way to learn a language, of course. . . . Daily usage. . . .

Pause. CATHERINE sings suddenly.

CATHERINE: *very loud*
"What makes a lady of eighty go out on the loose?"

MARGARET: Oh, stop it!

EVE: Where's your little girl? Where's Joan?

CATHERINE: She's asleep.

MARGARET: Not for long.

CATHERINE: She sleeps through everything. She sleeps all the time. Sometimes I — I hate her — being able to sleep like that.

MARGARET: *as CATHERINE staggers* You're going to fall down!

CATHERINE: I never fall down!

MARTA: My grandfather — he could drink and dance all
    night long. And he'd never even seem tipsy! Then
    suddenly his eyes would close, he'd go stiff as a board,
    and he'd fall down — boom! Flat on the floor!
    Sometimes he'd lie there for eighteen or twenty hours.
    Without moving, without making a sound. In the middle
    of the floor!

MARTA, CATHERINE and EVE laugh.

EVE: *now a bit tipsy herself*   Boom!

MARTA: Yes!

EVE: Where was that?

MARTA: That was — in Germany.

MARGARET: Germany! You've got a lot of gall, talking
    about Germany at a time like this!   *Indicating
    CATHERINE.*   Her husband's over there somewhere.

MARTA: In Germany?

EVE: No, no, he's missing in *France*!   *To CATHERINE.*
    Billy's battalion was at Dieppe, wasn't it? Dieppe is in
    France!

CATHERINE: It used to be.

EVE: *taking another sip*   Di-*eppe*! Boy, that's a funny
    name! Di-*eppe*!

EVE, CATHERINE and MARTA laugh.

MARGARET: I can't believe you're sitting here talking
    about it like — like it was a nice spot for a Sunday
    picnic! We all know what happened over there!

CATHERINE: *putting her arm around MARGARET again* I think you'd feel better if you had something to drink.

MARGARET: I've asked for coffee five times! Don't you have any coffee?

CATHERINE: I don't know.

MARGARET: Do you mind if I have a look?

CATHERINE: "Feel free." Billy always says that. *Suggestively.* "Feel free." I won't tell you *when* he says it.

The others laugh, except MARGARET who goes out, disgusted, in search of coffee.

CATHERINE: How old *is* that woman? Doesn't anybody know? I'll start the guessing at three hundred and fifty!

They laugh. Pause. They drink and smoke.

EVE: All the men in Harry's family were in one war or another. Except Harry. When I can't stand him any longer, I remind him of that fact. You should see. He crumples up like an old brown paper bag — goes and sits and stares at his gun collection. He'll fight about anything. Except that.

Pause.

CATHERINE: When Billy and I were first married, we fought all the time. Sometimes we'd stay up all night, fighting. Great times! *She drinks.* My mother hated him. I guess she still does. Is it legal to hate a Canadian soldier?

Pause.

MARTA: *singing, very slowly*
"The hurdy-gurdies, the birdies, the cop on the beat,
The candy-maker, the baker —"

MARGARET returns.

MARGARET: I couldn't find any coffee. I'm making some Ovaltine. Anybody else want some Ovaltine?

MARTA: What is it?

MARGARET: *Ovaltine.* It's very popular in our country. We drink it all the time.

MARTA: *I* don't drink it.

MARGARET: Why don't you go home?   *Indicating CATHERINE.*   Can't you see you're making her miserable?

CATHERINE, off in her own thoughts, is giggling quietly.

MARTA: No. I can't see that.

MARGARET: Imagine what she must think about when she looks at you.

MARTA: She's not looking at me.

MARGARET moves away.

MARTA: *singing*   "The hurdy-gurdies, the birdies —"

CATHERINE: *starting a little louder than she intends to*
There's this man —! There's this man, out at the plant. I like the way he — Did I tell you this already?

EVE: No.

CATHERINE: There's this man. Out at the plant. I don't know his name. Jim. Jim Somebody. Every night after work, he asks me to go out with him. Somewhere. And every night, I say "no."

MARGARET: I should hope so!

CATHERINE: But I — I like the way he looks. He must be about forty-five. Forty-six. Tall. Very black hair. I like the way he looks. Nothing wrong with that. Is there?

EVE: *quite tipsy* Absolutely not.

CATHERINE: I don't think I like the way he looks as much as I like the way Billy looks. *Pause.* But sometimes I don't remember — exactly — how Billy looks. He doesn't look like any of his pictures, I remember that. He doesn't take a good picture. *Pause.* The only picture of him I like is one I took four or five years ago — our holiday on the West Coast. He's wearing this ratty old sweater — I should've made him throw that thing out! Big enough for two of him! And he's stooping over to pick up a sand crab. And then — the crab bit him! *She laughs.* I wish I could've got *that* on film! *Pause.* You can't actually see Billy's face in the picture. His face is — in shadow. I'm a lousy photographer. But it looks like him anyway. Isn't that — peculiar?

Pause.

EVE: I read somewhere they may bomb the West Coast.

MARGARET: Who?

EVE: The Japanese.

MARGARET: Nonsense.

EVE: My Grade 10's made little buttons to wear that
       say: "Zap the Jap." I told them: "Take those off!"
       But they complained to the principal and he gave them
       permission to wear them. He's just like Harry. Old and
       stupid.

Pause.

CATHERINE: *sings*
       "The city charmer, the farmer, the Man in the Moon —"
       Very quietly.   Yesterday afternoon — I nearly didn't
       say "no."

EVE: What?

CATHERINE: I nearly didn't say "no."

MARGARET: What are you talking about?

CATHERINE: *I nearly didn't say "no!"* Yesterday
       afternoon. To Jim! Jim — Somebody.

MARGARET: Well, I think that's terrible!

EVE: Shhh!

MARGARET: Don't "shhh" me! I think it's *terrible*!

CATHERINE: So do I.   *Pause.*   When Billy and I
       were first married — we fought all the time. About
       everything. My clothes. His clothes. My friends. His
       friends. Whether or not to have children. How many
       to have. Girls or boys. We fought about baseball teams,
       which I didn't know anything about. We fought about
       religion and politics, which neither of us knew anything
       about. We fought about whether or not it was healthy
       for us to fight so much.   *Pause.*   One day — we'd
       only been married a few months — Billy borrowed some
       rope and came home from work early. I was having a
       nap. When I woke up, I was bound — hand and foot!
       I couldn't move an inch! And Billy was standing there —

61

grinning like a halfwit. "From now on," he said, "no more fighting. We're going to make love instead. Whenever we feel a fight coming on, we're going to make love instead. And if you don't agree, I'm going to strangle you and dump your remains in the river!"

She laughs.

MARGARET: I don't see anything very amusing about that.

Pause.

CATHERINE: When I think about those times, I can almost see Billy again. At least, I can see his eyes. I can see his hands. And his teeth. He has perfect teeth. Not like mine. That's something else we fought about. *Pause.* But the rest of the picture — is in shadow. *Pause.* Listen. If they want to make the Hollywood blockbuster of all time — one of those stories of tragic romance — sure to have every woman in the theatre reaching for her hanky — they should tell the story of a woman — whose husband goes away — but he goes away, one piece at a time. First an arm vanishes. Then a leg. Then his eyes. His hands. His teeth. Finally she can't remember what he looked like — at all.   *Pause.* That's what hurts.   *Pause.*   That's what's — peculiar. *Pause.*   Losing him — a little at a time.   *Pause.* *She sings:*

"Why are the stars always winkin' and blinkin' above?"

To MARTA.   That's how it starts!   *She sings:*

"Why are the stars always winkin' and blinkin' above What makes a fella start thinkin' —?"

She passes out, falls down flat on the floor. MARGARET and EVE rush to her.

MARTA: That's exactly how my grandfather did it!

"Elmer's Tune" is heard.

Interval.

Scene Fifteen

EVE stands alone, angry. She speaks to the audience.

EVE: I always said politicians are a little lower than one-
celled parasites in the natural order of things. But I
never thought the Prime Minister of Canada would renege
on a promise made to his people. No matter how many
stupid people wanted him to! Now they can call up
whomever they like, whenever they like! Farm boys,
law office clerks, college students. Call them all up!
Take them all!   Pause.   Of course, Harry was dancing
on air. "That goddamn, softhearted Scotsman finally
woke up to the fact there's a war on! And that means
manpower! That means bodies!" Yes, Harry. That means
bodies on top of more bodies on top of more bodies.
Pause.   I didn't put any sugar in his grapefruit juice
this morning. He hates that. It makes his whole face
pucker up. I said, "It was an accident, Harry."   *Pause.*
It wasn't.

*The lights come up immediately on the next scene, for which
EVE is already in position.*

Scene Sixteen

At one side of the stage, near a light switch, JANET is standing, holding a stop watch and a flashlight. Also near her are a large coat-tree and a long folding table.

On the other side of the stage are MARGARET and CATHERINE, hats, coats and shoes properly on, each holding a small paper bag, stuffed with various medical and personal "necessities."

In the middle of the stage is EVE, only one shoe on, her hat tucked under one arm, her coat slung precariously over her shoulders, her paper bag dangling, empty, from one hand. Her "necessities" are strewn across the folding table, and under it. Her other shoe is still under the coat-tree, near JANET. JANET is glaring at her.

JANET: *Now.* Shall we try it just one more time?

EVE: I'm sorry. I really am sorry.

JANET: Concentration! That's what it's all about.

As JANET continues her speech, MARGARET, CATHERINE and EVE cross to replace their hats and coats on the coat-tree. They remove their shoes and place them under the coat-tree, then dump the contents of their paper bags (in EVE's case, nothing) onto the folding table. MARGARET and CATHERINE cross back to the opposite side of the stage, with their paper bags. EVE follows them, after re-arranging her "necessities" on the table.

JANET: *to EVE, continuing her speech*   You won't prove anything to us, or to yourself, mooning around about Harry. Or whatever. Preparation. Organization. Concentration. That's what it's all about.   *She pauses, as the others line up on the opposite side of the stage.* Is everybody ready now?

MARGARET: Let's get it over with.

CATHERINE: I have to be home in half an hour. My
    babysitter's a high school girl.

JANET: *looking at her stop watch*   Everybody ready?
    Set?

EVE: *tentatively*   Yes.

JANET: *her hand on the light switch*   Then —
    blackout!

*She switches off the lights, switches on her flashlight, holds
it close to the stop watch, counting the seconds. She doesn't
move.*

*In the darkness (which is "theatrical" not literal),
MARGARET, EVE and CATHERINE race for the coat-tree.
They can be dimly perceived, scrambling into coats, hats,
etc., rummaging around on the table, filling the paper bags
with their "necessities." There is much noise and movement,
which diminishes gradually.*

JANET: *during the above, shouting*   Work quickly but
    work *carefully*!

EVE: *Carefully!*

JANET: Make up your mind you're going to accomplish
    the task, and then *accomplish it*!

Fifteen seconds pass. The noise has diminished considerably.

JANET: *her hand on the switch again*   Your — time —
    is — *up*!

*She switches on the lights. MARGARET and CATHERINE
have put on shoes, hats, coats, and have filled their paper
bags with all their "necessities" from the table. They have
moved back to their original positions.*

EVE is still by the coat-tree, only a few articles spilling out of her paper bag, no hat, no shoes, one arm through her coat, which is wrong-side-out. The others look at her. CATHERINE and MARGARET smile, shake their heads. JANET looks at EVE, sighs and crosses to MARGARET.

JANET: *inspecting MARGARET's clothing, etc.*
   Good. This is good work.

MARGARET: *not thrilled*   Thank you.

JANET: Properly organized and planned. You've been practicing at home.

MARGARET: What else have I got to do?

CATHERINE: Don't start that again.

MARGARET: I wasn't talking to you.

JANET: *looking at MARGARET's paper bag*   I don't see your aspirin. You didn't forget your aspirin?

MARGARET: I didn't forget anything.   *She takes the bag from JANET, rummages through it, takes out several small articles.*   Toothpaste. Pocket knife. Matches. Heavy stockings.   *She takes out a little bottle.*   Aspirin!

JANET: Excellent. Nice to know some of us will be prepared, if and when that awful day arrives.

MARGARET: *not thrilled*   Thank you.

JANET inspects CATHERINE's clothing, paper bag, etc.

JANET: Good, good. We're turning this into a fine art, aren't we? *Some of us.*

She glares at EVE, then crosses to her.

EVE: I'm sorry. I couldn't seem to find — I didn't know which —

JANET: *waving EVE's nearly empty bag* What's this?

EVE: My air raid evacuation parcel.

JANET: Well, you could've fooled me.

MARGARET: Don't be so hard on her. She's doing her best.

JANET: Obviously we'll have to try it once again. From the top. Till *everyone* gets it right!

CATHERINE and MARGARET groan. During the ensuing conversation, they cross back to the table, dump the contents of their paper bags onto it, take off their hats and coats, hang them on the coat-tree, then place their shoes underneath it. EVE follows suit, trying hard to organize her paraphernalia in advance.

EVE: I've been practicing too. Every night. But I can't seem to concentrate in the dark. I never could.

JANET: Ask yourself one question. What if this were the real thing — an enemy attack — a genuine "lights out and evacuate?" What would you do?

EVE: I'd — I'd —

JANET: Would you expect a neighbour — or your poor husband — to gather up your essentials for you?

EVE: No!

CATHERINE: It doesn't help to nag her to death. My God!

JANET: I am concerned! That's all. Concerned for *her*. Didn't we agree the only way to be ready for this emergency is to rehearse it? Know what your essentials are and where they are, get them together, and get out!

MARGARET: If we're doing it again, let's do it.

CATHERINE: *a private joke*   "Let's do it!"

JANET: This exercise has been approved by the Red Cross and the Kinsmen, you know.

CATHERINE: We know.

MARGARET and CATHERINE have crossed to their original positions, paper bags in hand. EVE joins them.

EVE: I said I'm sorry.

JANET: "Sorry" won't save your life, if and when that awful day arrives. *Now*, are we all ready again? Set?

EVE: *determined*   Yes.

JANET: *her hand on the light switch*   Then — *blackout!*

Lights out, flashlight on, JANET focusses on her stop watch. Business as before. Much noise is heard.

JANET: Use your wits! That's what they're there for!

EVE: *somewhere, invisible*   *Ow!*

JANET: Do not panic!

CATHERINE: Are you okay?

JANET: Panic never helped anybody!

Fifteen seconds pass.

JANET: Your — time — is —

EVE: Oh no.

JANET: *Up!*

She switches on the lights. The situation is nearly identical: CATHERINE and MARGARET in shoes, hats, coats, organized; EVE, possibly a little worse than before. The others look at her.

EVE: I couldn't find one of my shoes! It wasn't there! I looked, but it wasn't there!

JANET points. EVE looks down to discover the missing shoe in her own hand.

EVE: Oh no.

CATHERINE laughs.

JANET: *One more time?*

EVE: What's the use?

JANET: I'm inclined to agree. But we started this, I want us all to finish it, if possible.   *To EVE.*   Don't you realize you might have to face the grim reality of this test, any day now?

MARGARET: Nonsense.

JANET: It isn't nonsense!

MARGARET: Well, it's not very likely, is it?

JANET: I'll tell you exactly what I told my husband. "Let them call me a pessimist, or worse. Let them laugh at me for putting up blackout curtains and knowing my evacuation route. They won't find so much to laugh about, if the fire bombs start to rain down on us here, like they have on London." Some of the British thought these exercises were a lark too. They discovered otherwise. *Too late.*

CATHERINE. Oh, come on! We're thousands of miles from the Germans, almost as far from the Japanese. Emergency training is one thing, but what's the point of scaring ourselves to death?

MARGARET: She's right.

JANET: Is she? And what if they launch an attack from Alaska?

CATHERINE: *Alaska?*

JANET: *Alaska.*

CATHERINE: Who?

JANET: The bloody Japanese! You think the Americans are building their highway into the frozen North for the fun of it? They know. *They know.*

CATHERINE: There aren't any airfields in Alaska.

MARGARET: Nor much else as far as I ever heard.

JANET: This is the twentieth century! The age of modern science! They can build an airfield overnight if they want to! *Looking at CATHERINE.* God! Ignorant and naïve women may seem charming in peacetime, but in times like these, they're just plain dangerous! *Slight pause.* Enough said. Let's do it again. From the top.

MARGARET and EVE cross toward the table. CATHERINE doesn't move.

CATHERINE: *to JANET, quietly*   You're a dried-up, self-important little bitch. Or is that being too naïve?

MARGARET: Oh Lord —

JANET: *after taking a moment to recover*   Let me remind you —

CATHERINE: That you're in charge here? No need for that. You're in charge *everywhere*!

JANET: Look, I don't care what you think about me personally! This isn't the time or place for —

CATHERINE: I said you're a bitch! That's what I think of you. That's what I've always thought of you, and this seems like the perfect time to let you know it!

Pause. CATHERINE and JANET stare at each other. MARGARET turns away. EVE shifts nervously from one foot to the other.

JANET: *tightly*   All right then. I'm sorry you feel this way. Truly. But I won't allow us to descend to personalities. What's at stake here is more important than —

CATHERINE: Oh hell! *Descend* from your bloody cloud for a minute, woman! Your wings need oiling!

Pause. JANET clinches her teeth, pockets her stop watch.

JANET: All right then. I will wait until you finish this — this attack.   *Pause. Softly but emphatically.*
I can't say I enjoy being insulted by someone who can't even remember that she's married, but all right!

EVE: *catching CATHERINE's look*   No! Please —

CATHERINE: *to JANET*   What the hell do you mean by that?!

JANET: Oh, you're not *that* naïve! I mean, maybe it's just your way of being patriotic — keeping the guys down at the munitions plant happy. It's not my idea of a significant contribution to democracy but — if you're really that lonely —

CATHERINE rips off her hat, throws it down, crosses to JANET, peeling off her coat.

EVE: No!

CATHERINE: *to JANET*   That's one subject I'd avoid if I were you!   *She throws her coat down too.* Loneliness! You think you know what it's like? Sitting at home, thinking about your husband, a million miles away? In a camp somewhere? In a wire cage! Oh no! Your little husband very wisely decided not to expose himself to the — inconveniences — of this little war! Didn't he?

JANET: He wanted to go! Desperately! But he's part of an "essential service!" He can't just abandon his work and —

CATHERINE: His work? Christ, he's a *voice*, that's his work! A voice that reads the radio news twice a day! There are plenty of older men and younger men and women who could read the news, for God's sake!

They are eye to eye. Pause.

JANET: *All right then.* I'm sure —when you realize how unfair — and stupid! — that accusation is — you'll want to apologize.

Pause.

CATHERINE: Bitch.

Pause.

JANET: Well — you're common.

CATHERINE: Do-gooder!

JANET: Tramp!

CATHERINE: You're a clown!

JANET: You're a whore!

*CATHERINE slaps her, hard. JANET grabs CATHERINE by
the front of her dress. CATHERINE grabs JANET. Pause.
CATHERINE lets go. JANET lets go. No one moves. Pause.*

MARGARET: *finally*   If you two have finished this
     beer parlour brawl, can we get back to what we came
     here for? I have nobody — nothing to go home to. But
     I'd rather be there than here, watching this!

EVE: Maybe we should — call a halt — for today?

Pause.

JANET: *very tightly*   *No.* We mustn't waste any more
     time on — personalities. Not in times like these.
     She looks CATHERINE in the eye.   I'm willing to
     say — I'm sorry — if you're willing to do the same.
     For the sake of — the activity at hand?

*Pause. CATHERINE says nothing. She crosses, dumps the
contents of her paper bag on the long table, picks up her hat
and coat, hangs them on the coat-tree, leaves her shoes
underneath it, crosses to the opposite side of the stage.
MARGARET and EVE quickly perform similar business and
join her, paper bags in hand. They all turn and look at
JANET.*

JANET: *after a considerable pause, in a small, tight*
  voice Good. Are we all ready now? Set?

EVE: *faintly* . . . Yes . . .

JANET: *fiercely, her hand on the light switch* Then —
  BLACKOUT!!

*A real blackout. JANET does not switch on her flashlight.
There is no sound for several seconds.*

Scene Seventeen

*A long, shrill blast on a military siren is heard. A spotlight
comes up slowly on MARTA, who is alone. She speaks to
the audience.*

MARTA: They have graduated from smoke bombs, and
  swastikas scrawled on the windows with soap, and a
  mail box full of sauerkraut. When I went out for the
  morning paper, there was a dead dog on the front steps.
  A large black dog. It had been dead for about a week, I
  guess. Of course, today is a very special day.

*The spotlight stays on her. Another long, shrill blast on
a military siren is heard, then a man's voice barks an
unintelligible command. At the same time, another spotlight
comes up slowly on MARGARET, who is alone, kneeling.*

MARGARET: Our Father which art in Heaven . . . I went
  downtown today, Lord, to raise my voice and send my
  prayers to you. Along with all the others who gathered
  at the corner of Centre Street. The sidewalk was hot.
  But I knelt down, just the same. I prayed for every man
  who'll be crawling up that awful beach. And I said thanks
  that my sons aren't there. Oh yes, lost to me forever —
  both of them. But not there, at least. Not today.

The spotlight stays on her. Another long, shrill blast on a military siren is heard, then a man's voice barks an unintelligible command, which is answered by many shouts from farther away. At the same time, another spotlight comes up slowly on JANET, who is alone. She speaks to the audience.

JANET: On each table I want a small arrangement of red geraniums, white asters and blue cornflowers, surrounding a vase of Union Jacks. Cheerful but not gaudy. Women all over North America will be asking a few close friends to share their "D-Day Vigil." I've asked only twenty-five, and I'm serving no alcohol till after nine-thirty. My husband wanted to invite some people from the station. "Absolutely not," I told him, "you're not turning this solemn occasion into one of your parties!"

She smiles.

The spotlight stays on her. Another long, shrill blast on a military siren is heard, then a man's voice barks an unintelligible command which is answered by many shouts from farther away. Nearby, a tank motor suddenly grinds into gear. At the same time, another spotlight comes up slowly on CATHERINE, who is alone. She speaks to the audience.

CATHERINE: Jim's taking me somewhere called the Palace of Eats. With my luck, it'll probably live up to that name. He says he'll introduce me to the mad Greek that runs the place. Then a movie. Maybe over to Penley's for a dance or two. I don't give a damn what anybody thinks! Jim says, "Everybody's celebrating tonight. It's the beginning of the end of this stupid war. Your husband's not in Normandy, is he? You can celebrate that."

The spotlight stays on her. Another long, shrill blast on
a military siren is heard, then a man's voice barks an
unintelligible command, which is answered by many shouts
from farther away. Nearby, a tank motor suddenly grinds
into gear. A burst of machine gun fire is heard. At the same
time, another spotlight comes up slowly on EVE, who is
alone. She speaks to the audience.

EVE: I knew he'd drive me to it. Sooner or later.
    We were listening to some insane radio announcer,
    trying to conjure up for us the emotions of men going
    into combat. Harry sneered at me: "Yes, and there'd
    be more of our boys rushing those Nazi bastards, if you
    and your kind didn't talk them into staying in school!
    They'll take a kid of sixteen now, if he lies a little!"
    I went straight to the gun cabinet and took out a thirty-
    ought-six Winchester rifle. Harry made me memorize
    the names of his guns. And then I took aim. "You know
    that's loaded?" he said. "Oh yes," I said, "I intend to
    prove that it is, if you don't shut up and clear out of here
    for a while!" I sounded like Randolph Scott. Then I
    cocked the hammer. I don't know where Harry is tonight.
    I don't care where he is.

The spotlight stays on her. Another long, shrill blast on
a military siren is heard, then a man's voice barks an
unintelligible command, which is answered by many shouts
from farther away. Nearby, a tank motor suddenly grinds
into gear. A burst of machine gun fire is heard.

Now the battle noise continues — building, building — more
and more various noises being added to the din.

As the noise crescendos, the women slowly, separately leave
their individual spotlights and converge in the semi-darkness,
centre stage.

As the battle sounds reach a deafening fortissimo, the
spotlights fade and a very brilliant hot light comes up on
the huddle of women, centre stage — tightly grouped, facing
out into the darkness, terrified but still.

Suddenly the battle sounds cease. There are several seconds of silence. The women do not move.

There is a real blackout. Pause.

In the darkness, JANET begins to play a sad tune on the upright.

Scene Eighteen

The lights come up. JANET is at the piano. She sings to herself.

JANET: *singing*
 "Now is the hour when we must say goodbye.
 Soon you'll be sailing, far across the sea.
 While you're away, O then remember me!
 When you return, you'll find me —"

She stops playing, speaks angrily to the audience, as though to another individual.

JANET: Idiot. You idiot! Who the hell do you think
 I've been doing it *for*? Clubs, committees, collections,
 councils — you think I enjoyed it? I wanted you to be
 proud of me. I wanted them to respect both of us! Now
 I realize they've been laughing at me. All this time. And
 you've been laughing hardest of all — haven't you?
 You and — No, I won't even speak her name!

She plays again.

JANET: *singing*
 "Now is the hour when we must say goodbye.
 Soon you'll be sailing —"

She stops playing, speaks downstage to "him," as before.

JANET: Why don't you say something? Why don't you
    try to explain? Or apologize? I'd love to hear that! Why
    don't you tell me — while I was out knitting socks and
    teaching the tango to artillery sergeants — go on, tell
    me! — where were you? And who were you with? . . .
    Don't bother. *Don't bother.*

She plays again.

JANET: *singing*
    "Now is the hour when we must say good —"

She stops playing.

JANET: *speaking to "him," as before*   You're a liar!
    Pause.   And I said to myself: "No. No, they won't
    despise him for not going, for not volunteering. Not if
    I'm doing all I can, here at home. I'll just have to work
    harder, do more and care more than any of them. For
    his sake!"   *Pause.*   And really, she's — she's not
    even pretty!

She plays again.

JANET: *singing*   "Now is the hour —"

She stops playing.

JANET: *speaking to "him," as before*   Because I
    happen to *love* this old song, that's why! And because
    I have to teach it to the whole gang down at the
    Fireside Sing-Along tonight, that's why!   *Pause.*
    Quietly.   You son of a bitch.

*She starts playing again, bearing down very hard on the
keys.*

JANET: *singing*
    "Now is the hour when we must say goodbye —"

Her voice cracks. She stops singing but finishes playing the chorus of the song. The final bars of this chorus overlap with airplane sounds as the next scene begins.

Scene Nineteen

MARTA, EVE and CATHERINE.

A blanket is spread out on the ground. The women have picnic hampers with them. The occasional sound of airplanes overhead is heard. EVE, with a pair of binoculars, watches the planes. CATHERINE, stretched out on the blanket, half asleep, suns herself. MARTA eats a sandwich.

MARTA: And he'll be home again next Saturday, they said.

EVE: You must be ecstatic.

MARTA: I don't understand. They lock him up for all these years. Like he was a master spy. He's sixty years old! Now they turn him loose. There's still a war on. He still gives tobacco to the German P.O.W.'s. He hasn't lost his accent. Or his opinions. But they send him home. They don't give any reasons.

CATHERINE: Probably they don't have any. Everybody's gone a little wacky.

EVE: *observing the planes*   Wonderful!

MARTA: *to CATHERINE*   Oh, more than a little. Somebody told me an old man in Medicine Hat chopped off three of his toes. Because they were grafted onto him from a dead German soldier in the last war. He said, "I don't want any Nazi toes."

CATHERINE: Not seriously?

MARTA: Yes.

CATHERINE: My God.

EVE: Here comes the entire formation! Beautiful!
They're doing those Mosquito Squadron manoeuvres.
Loop-the-loops, nose dives! Can you see them?

CATHERINE: I've seen them before.

EVE: You have to find beauty wherever you can
nowadays. Even when you don't particularly approve
of the source.

Pause.

MARTA: And now they send him home! No, I'm not
ecstatic. He's gone even crazier while he was away. I
went to see him last week. He told me he knows I'm
not really his daughter. He knows I'm somebody the
Canadian Intelligence dressed up and taught to speak
like his daughter. To spy on him. "But I don't know
anything," he said. He grabbed me and he held me so
close! "I swear to you — whoever you are — I don't
know *anything!*"

CATHERINE: He might get over that, when he's been
home a while.

EVE: *looking through the binoculars*   Breathtaking!

MARTA: Then he pointed to a little bush out in the
middle of the field — the fenced-off field where the
prisoners are allowed to exercise. And he said, "That's
my caragana bush. That's all I'm telling you. That's the
only secret I have from them here. So if they find me,
next time I drop down and hide behind my caragana
bush, I'll know *you* told them. I'll know you're not my
daughter!" The way he laughed. . . .

She shakes her head.

EVE: He wouldn't hurt you, would he? After he comes back?

MARTA: No. I don't think so.

Pause.

MARTA: *to CATHERINE*   What's happening to Billy now?

CATHERINE: He's joined a new regiment. On the clean-up campaign. France or Belgium or Luxembourg. God knows where. There's a lot of cleaning up to be done. He says the food's worse in his regiment than it was in the German camp.

MARTA: But he thinks he'll be all right now.

CATHERINE: He never doubted he'd be all right. That's Billy.

EVE suddenly leaps to her feet and screams, still staring through the binoculars.

EVE: *No!*

CATHERINE: What is it?

EVE: *takes a deep breath*   I swear to you, he didn't miss the flagpole on the hotel by more than three or four inches!

CATHERINE: Probably looked closer than it was.

EVE: Five — five and a half inches at the most!

CATHERINE: Why do you watch them if it scares you?

EVE: Well, I've taken a greater interest in — aviation — ever since. . . .

CATHERINE: My God. Here we go.

EVE: I wanted to scream. When I saw his photograph in the paper. I just couldn't believe it! He was only fifty-three, you know. He had many more years and a wonderful career ahead of him.

CATHERINE: Didn't you tell me Harry's only fifty-one?

EVE: You're not seriously comparing Harry with Leslie Howard? Harry's older at fifty-one than Leslie Howard would've been at ninety-one.   *Pause.*   I asked the manager at the Grand if he'd be showing *Intermezzo* again.   *Pause.*   I felt like screaming. And Harry was walking on eggs for a week. He's anything but sensitive. But he knew not to trifle with me — after they found — what was left of Leslie Howard's plane.   *Pause.*   I'd better not talk about it anymore.

CATHERINE: I second that motion.

Pause.

MARTA: "I want my daughter there when I come home," my father said, "my real daughter. I'm not a fool! But I have to admit there's a strong resemblance." He isn't well. It's not only his mind. He was shaking. Like this. And he was. . . . Tears were coming from his eyes. You know? He wasn't crying, but there was water streaming down his face. He didn't even notice. I took out my handkerchief and gave it to him. He looked at it, then at me. He said, "This is poisoned, isn't it?" In a fairy tale he used to read to me, there was a poisoned handkerchief. He always loved that part, about the poisoned handkerchief.

EVE: *observing the planes again*   Amazing!

Pause.

CATHERINE: Jim said he'd marry me if he could. I laughed. I said, "I'm already married to somebody I like." "So am I," he said. Well, I knew that. I mean, he'd never said anything, but . . . "My God," I told him, "I knew that. You think my high school class elected me Miss Intuition for nothing?"

MARTA: You won't see him again?

CATHERINE: Not — seriously. We might go to the Shangri-La for one last fling. Or we might not.

MARTA: Will you miss him?

CATHERINE: Not much. Not when Billy's home.

MARTA: But he's nothing like Billy, you told me.

CATHERINE: The change will be nice. *Pause.* I guess maybe I *do* think like a whore. You think I do?

MARTA: I don't think about people that way. I just think, "So that's how she manages to stay alive. I wonder if it would work for me."

CATHERINE: Pass me a sandwich?

EVE: *offering her binoculars*   You girls should take a turn behind these things. It'll change your whole perspective. Man subdues the elements and the law of gravity! *Pause.*   My poor Leslie Howard. You won't ever be dead, as far as I'm concerned.

CATHERINE eats a sandwich, lying back in the sun again.
MARTA takes an apple from the hamper, bites into it.
Pause.

EVE: Thursday in class, one of the boys — a staunch
cadet — told me he knows I'm a subversive. "You'll
be glad when the war's over," he said, "won't you?
No matter who wins." "Yes," I told him, "I'll be
ecstatic!" "We ought to drag you out," he said, "stand
you against a wall, and see how many holes we could
put through you!"

She makes a loud machine gun noise.

Pause. She returns to observing the planes.

Scene Twenty

*MARGARET is alone, in her slip, painting her legs. She
speaks to the audience.*

MARGARET: I'm tired of being old. It's only a state of
mind. I don't feel old. Not that old. Even our minister's
wife went out and bought herself one of those new longer
skirts — and a sweater — and she's sixty if she's a day!
I'll be alone the rest of my life. Unless I get out, meet
some people.   *She looks at her legs.*   Can't tell it
from the real thing.   *She has a sudden stitch in her
side, takes a deep breath, sits down. Pause. She relaxes
a bit.*   People die when they're alone all the time.
They die of diseases that don't exist.   *Pause.*   I
wonder what they'd all say — if I got married again?
Pause.   Of course, if my next one was anything like my
last one, it might be better to be dead than married again.
*Pause. She takes a deep breath, stands and continues her
leg-painting.*   I took the bus up North. Rode all night
long. When I got to the pen, they told me he didn't want
to see me. Then they came back and said, "It's all right.
We persuaded him." I'm afraid they shouted at him —
or roughed him up. Anyway he came out. We had a talk.
Not long and not pleasant. I asked him, "Why are you so
thin?" He just stared at me. Then he said, "Why are you
so fat, Mother?"   *Pause.*   I have put on a few

pounds. There's nobody else to eat it all — tomato pickles and preserves and potatoes. Can't pay my rent half the time, but I eat like royalty. All these years they've been telling us, "Put everything away, grow everything yourself, save everything! This country could be at starvation's door tomorrow!" Now I have a cellar full of food that nobody wants.

She finishes painting her legs, sits and stretches painfully.

MARGARET: No letter from Halifax for six weeks. Oh, they said things were looking brighter over there. But I know what this silence means. Both of them. Gone forever.   *Pause.*   Lord. He looked so thin in that huge cold room. His arms — from the elbow up — were no bigger around than — than my wrist!   *Pause. She cries out.   I can't be alone here!   Pause.*   I know what happens to people who are alone.

She stands, determined, picks up an eyebrow pencil and starts to put on her "seams."

The "Beer Barrel Polka" fades up, slowly.

MARGARET: I'll throw myself into it, meet some other people. Get away from — all this. It's only a state of mind.

The polka continues, rather loud, throughout most of the next scene.

Scene Twenty~One

A Red Cross box with bandages neatly packed inside it is seen.

EVE alone, crosses to the box, reaches inside and carefully takes out a bandage. Then suddenly she screams happily and tosses the bandage into the air, unfurling it like a streamer at a parade. She laughs. She takes out another bandage, screams and unfurls it, laughing.

JANET joins her, furious.

JANET: What in God's name? —

EVE: It's over!

JANET: What?

EVE: *It's over!*

She takes out another bandage, screams, unfurls it.

JANET: *pushing her away from the box*   Have you lost your mind?

EVE: *breathless*   Didn't you hear? The treaty! —

JANET: There is still a war on!

She retrieves the bandages that EVE has scattered and folds them.

EVE: Signed, sealed and delivered! Eisenhower signed it and — and all the rest of them!

JANET: Listen to me —

EVE: Four days from now — midnight! — "all quiet on the Western Front!"

JANET: But *there is still a war on*! In the Pacific!

EVE: Oh, that can't last much longer now!

She grabs JANET impulsively and kisses her.

JANET: Stop that!

CATHERINE joins them.

JANET: *seeing her* Thank God! *Indicating EVE.* She's lost her mind!

CATHERINE: *to EVE* You heard?

EVE: It's over!

CATHERINE: *Yes!* *They embrace.* Two old men were dancing together in the street outside my house. The younger one must've been about eighty. I said, "What's happening?" The older one hit me with his newspaper: "How's those for headlines, sister?!" And the younger one just kept screaming, "Ding-dong, ding-dong, ding-dong!"

EVE: Ding-dong!

CATHERINE: He said, "I'm the first bell in this goddamn city to find its tongue!"

EVE: Ding-dong!

JANET: *to EVE* Sit down!

EVE: Ding-dong!

JANET: *to CATHERINE* Make her sit down!

CATHERINE: Ding-dong!

EVE: *beside herself with joy*   It's over! No more "fire over England!" No more "guts and grit!" *It's over! How's that for scuttlebutt, Harry?!*

CATHERINE: Ding-dong!

EVE: Ding-dong!!

JANET: *Stop it!*

CATHERINE: *to JANET*   Oh, for God's sake! Can't you even enjoy *this*!

JANET: The war is not over! What about the Japanese? *She still gathers up bandages.*   A lot of time and effort went into organizing — all this! —

She is in tears.

CATHERINE: *grabbing her*   Forget about the bloody Japanese! Forget about all your time and effort! Be a little happy at least! For us! For all of us! We *lasted*! We *made it*! Like the old man said: "Ding-dong — goddamnit! — ding-dong!!"

EVE: Ding-dong!!

MARGARET joins them, out of breath.

MARGARET: You heard?

EVE: Ding-dong!

She embraces MARGARET. So does CATHERINE.

MARGARET: I didn't know whether to believe it or not!

CATHERINE: It's been on the radio all morning!   *To JANET.*   Your husband! Your husband was on, shouting and singing and crying —

JANET: *quietly* Don't talk to me about him!

She moves away from the others.

CATHERINE: It's over!

EVE: *hanging on to MARGARET* You see? I told you you're a silly woman! All these years you spent weeping and wailing: "I'll never see my sons again!"

CATHERINE: Your boy could be home from Halifax any day now! And Billy —

EVE: *to MARGARET* And the other one! They won't keep him much longer! Surely not! Now that it's all over!

CATHERINE: And *Billy*!

MARGARET: You know what I think?

EVE: Ding-dong!

CATHERINE: Ding-dong!

JANET: This is absurd!

MARGARET: I think we should all get down on our knees —

EVE: Ding-dong!

MARGARET: And give thanks to God — whose mercy —

She has started to kneel. Suddenly she gasps, grabs her side and drops to her knees with a thud. JANET is the first to see this.

JANET: *screaming at CATHERINE and EVE* Stop it! *Rushing to MARGARET.* Oh my God.

MARGARET *remains on her knees, clutching her side,
unable to speak, her face contorted by pain.*

EVE: What? —

CATHERINE: What is it?

They rush to MARGARET.

JANET: *kneeling beside MARGARET*   I don't know!
I was afraid something like this would happen, all the
shouting and —   *Looking at MARGARET, to the
others.*   Get a doctor. Get somebody!

Blackout. Pause.

Scene Twenty~Two

CATHERINE, *in a black dress, a little nervous and very
rushed, is pawing her way through a black handbag.*

CATHERINE: Was it two-thirty or three? I thought it was
three.   *She takes a small address and memo book from
the bag, leafs through it and reads.*   "Little Chapel on
the Corner. Two-thirty!" My God, I'm going to be late.
She puts the book back in the bag.   Two-thirty!
*She picks up a small black hat with a veil and pins it on
her head.*   Everybody's rushing to do everything at
once, now that it's all over. I've been to more showers,
baptisms, weddings and funerals the past few weeks than
the rest of my life put together.   *Pause. She straightens
the hat, pins it again, checks it in a mirror.*   Well, she
hung on as long as possible. And she wrote a letter to
both her sons, while she was in the hospital. She wrote
to forgive them for leaving her all alone — and to tell them
how proud she was of both of them. But the nurse told
me there's nothing in the envelope but a blank, white
sheet of paper. She was delirious the last few days. She
wrote her letter with the wrong end of the pencil. With

the eraser.   *Pause.*   I'm going to be late!   *She grabs a black coat and puts it on.*   Last night I dreamed about Billy. Most of him had come back. His eyes. His teeth. Home again, the end of the month. My God, he'll be so proud of himself!

She laughs and hurries out.

Scene Twenty~Three

There is a large floral wreath lying on the ground.

CATHERINE, JANET and EVE gather round the wreath. They all wear black coats and hats with veils.

Pause. EVE sniffles, then starts to sing, pitched rather high.

EVE: *singing*
"I come to the garden alone,
While the —"

JANET: Please don't do that.

EVE: It was her favourite.

JANET: You already sang it once. At the Chapel.

CATHERINE: It might sound better now — without that organist.

JANET: I think we should try to be serious about this.

CATHERINE: I think we should go soon.

Pause.

EVE: Classic irony. That's how I'd describe it to my Grade 11's. They're just starting the *Illiad*. Classic irony.

JANET: How old was she? Really? Does anybody know?

CATHERINE: What difference does it make?

EVE: Classic irony. Now they're coming home again. Both of them. And she won't be here to see how mistaken all her pessimism was.

JANET: I'm sure she realized, before the end. Don't you think so?

EVE: Classic irony.

CATHERINE: We ought to go soon.

Pause.

CATHERINE: I have to learn to cook again. To make the bed and fold shirts. I lost all my good habits while Billy was gone.   *Pause.*   I have to learn to fight again.

EVE: You can come over and practice on Harry, if you like. He's more impossible than usual this week. Very excited about devastation. He always has been. He no longer greets me at breakfast with the mighty Bren. Now it's atomic explosions.

She makes the sound of an explosion.

JANET: Please. Let's try to remember where we are.

CATHERINE: We should go.

EVE: *to JANET*   What about your husband? Jack, isn't it? What's he up to these days?

JANET: *softly*   Why don't you shut up?

CATHERINE: Let's try to remember where we are.

Pause. They start out slowly. MARTA comes in, carrying a small potted plant. The others see her. Pause.

JANET hurries out, past MARTA. Pause.

EVE takes MARTA's hand, smiles feebly, then she goes out.

CATHERINE and MARTA embrace. CATHERINE touches MARTA's face for a moment, then she goes out. Pause.

MARTA moves downstage, glances at MARGARET's wreath, then crosses to the opposite side of the stage, and carefully sets her plant down. She recites quietly.

MARTA: *reciting*
"Vom Berg hinabgestiegen
ist nun des Tages Rest;
mein Kind liegt in der Wiegen,
die Vögel all im Nest.
Nur ein —
Nur ein kleines —   *Pause.*
Nur ein —"

It's no use. I can't remember it anymore. And it was your favourite, wasn't it? When I was three years old, I stood in front of your enormous chair to recite it. On your name-day.   *Pause.*   I have been thinking — what my life might have been. If you'd died two weeks before the war, instead of two weeks after. Screaming and kicking at me. To the last, I wasn't your daughter. "Some imposter they put in my home, to torture me!" You kept screaming and —   *Pause.*   Or if they'd never discovered your basement full of magazines — and your picture of the Führer at Berchtesgaden. . . . *Pause.*   I wonder if I could have become an Austrian overnight when the war was declared. So many of them did. Could I have left everything I have here, gone to another city? Could I have been more "anonymous?" *Anonymous.* Such a funny word.   *Pause.*   I remember. I was still in school. You and Mama had decided to improve your English vocabulary — to impress your friends. You asked me about "anonymous." And I said, "Oh, didn't you know? There's one of those right here in Calgary! In the zoo. One of the few in captivity!" So you invited several of your best customers to come with us on our family stroll that Sunday. "We're going down to the zoo," you told them, "to see the anonymous!" *Pause.* That story was repeated for months. People laughed. *Pause.* You hated me for nearly an entire year after that. You never had a sense of humour. Not much. *Pause.* It might have helped you, if you had.

Pause. She waits.

The Tauber record is heard, very, very far away.

TAUBER:
"Banger Gram, eh' sie kam,
Hat die Zukunft mit umhüllt,"
Etc.

The Tauber record fades as a snappier number jumps in; a swing tune similar to the number in Scene One, but maybe jazzier, more "1945," loud.

Scene Twenty~Four

The swing tune continues.

CATHERINE, JANET, EVE and MARTA are standing or seated, waiting.

JANET is standing, holding on to the back of a chair, moving her feet to the music. She is aggressively cheerful.

The others are motionless, moody or preoccupied. Pause. They wait.

Eventually JANET crosses to CATHERINE, taps her on the shoulder and nods towards the dance floor. CATHERINE shrugs and they move onto the dance floor together.

They dance for a moment. Both know the latest steps. Then CATHERINE suddenly steps away from JANET, crosses abruptly far downstage, into a bright light. She lifts her head, as though listening for something inaudible to everyone else. She waits.

JANET stares at CATHERINE, puzzled. She looks all around, finally crosses to EVE, taps her on the shoulder and nods towards the dance floor. EVE accepts reluctantly. She and JANET move onto the dance floor. CATHERINE has not moved.

JANET and EVE dance — the former, anxious but determined, smiling; the latter, nervous and unhappy, watching her feet.

While they dance, MARTA notices CATHERINE and crosses to join her, downstage, in the bright light. She stands near CATHERINE, slightly behind her. She also listens, and waits.

Pause.

JANET "spins" EVE. At this moment, EVE notices CATHERINE and MARTA. She starts towards them. JANET tries to draw her back, but EVE pulls free of her roughly and moves downstage. She takes CATHERINE's hand. CATHERINE looks at EVE for a moment, then back out into the darkness. EVE's eyes follow CATHERINE's.

JANET stares at them from upstage. She looks all around, lost.

For the first time now, a faint sound can be heard in the distance, underneath the swing tune. A rattle of drums is heard, exploding into a march, like a regiment of Canadian infantry about to hit the parade ground. This sound grows louder and louder, to the end of the scene.

Very slowly JANET moves downstage and joins the others. She stands slightly apart from them, but her eyes, like theirs, are focussed on the distance, the darkness.

The march swells and contends for a moment with the swing tune. After a moment, the march swamps the swing tune which fades quickly. The march continues.

The four women wait . . . wait . . . wait.

MARTA does not move.

JANET begins to shake her head, slightly but constantly from side to side, as though she can't believe what's happening.

Suddenly EVE bursts into loud sobs and covers her face with both hands.

Then CATHERINE recognizes someone "out there." Her hand shoots into the air, as though to wave or salute.

Blackout.

The march grows louder and louder.

Author's Note

I have intentionally kept stage directions to a minimum in this script. But, based on my observation of early productions, I suggest that the five characters remain onstage, perhaps dimly-lit upstage, or in specially designed "waiting areas," virtually throughout the play. This emphasizes the consistency and continuity of the action. It also allows the actresses to pick up on and continue the energy level of previous scenes, whether or not they were actually involved in them.

The production of the play by Northern Light Theatre in Edmonton, Alberta, managed to suggest, in a very simple setting, individual rooms in the homes of Catherine, Margaret, Janet and Marta, and Eve's office at school. Action appropriate to these rooms took place there, of course. But the women also "waited" in these vestigial rooms during scenes which did not include them. A large "neutral" area, stage centre, served as a dance hall, the Red Cross hut, the train station, the hillside above Calgary, the cemetery, etc. Especially in this simple setting, the play achieved the narrative "flow" which is so essential to its free structure.

Elaborate costume and hair-style changes, which might seem to contribute to the period atmosphere, actually detract in most cases from the cumulative energy of the "waiting." Whatever changes are necessary can usually be made onstage, if they are carefully lit and choreographed in rehearsal.

John Murrell,
Calgary, Alberta.
1980.

Appendix

The scene that follows was part of the original script and the original production of *Waiting for the Parade*. It occurred directly after the scene in Marta's shop (now Scene Nine) and before the train platform scene (now Scene Ten). Although the scene was effective, subsequent directors have felt that it lengthens an already long first part unnecessarily. They have also felt it may "violate" the all-female format of the script, which has men omnipresent but represented only in memory, in quotation, by suggestion, offstage characterization, etc. I include the scene here because I feel, somehow, that it still belongs to the text. In case any director should ever wish to reinstate it, I would not object, as long as it is performed in the slot originally designed for it.

Scene Nine "A"

CATHERINE is alone, standing beside a headless dressmaker's mannequin.

Pause. A VOICE is heard. CATHERINE stares at the mannequin for a while, not moving.

VOICE: *male, in his thirties*   Hello again, honey. Here I sit on the world's hardest bunk, in the world's leakiest tent. I can't get you off my mind today, which isn't unusual. Lots of nothing to write home about. Except this damned rain still hasn't let up, and that's no news either.

CATHERINE disappears for a moment, then returns with a shirt, jacket and necktie belonging to her husband.

VOICE: By the time I got those chocolate cookies they looked like they'd taken a torpedo amidships. The crumbs were delicious. I love you, honey. I taped the photo you sent of Ann Sheridan inside my foot locker, beside my only picture of you.

CATHERINE puts the shirt on the mannequin and buttons it up.

VOICE: Honest to God, I can't see much difference between you two. Except maybe you're a little prettier. That's a joke. In my book you're a hotter item than Ann Sheridan, any day.

CATHERINE puts the necktie around her own neck and carefully ties it.

VOICE: How's our Joan? I don't know how the two of you can manage on what they send from Ottawa. I wish they paid us better to sit around, soak up the English atmosphere and go to target practice twice a day. I keep telling them, those targets are never going to surrender.

CATHERINE loosens the tie, slips it off over her head and puts it on the mannequin.

VOICE: Did you get any more money from your mother? Don't ask her for any. But if she sends some, don't be too proud to keep it.

CATHERINE puts the jacket around the mannequin's shoulders.

VOICE: I know we always used to send her cheques back, the same day we got them. Things have changed. There's a war on. Or hadn't you heard?

CATHERINE steps back from the mannequin and stares at it.

VOICE: I love you, honey. *Pause.* The guy in the bunk across from mine, his name's Teddy. He's the biggest idiot in this man's army — and that's saying a lot.

CATHERINE steps forward, removes the jacket from the mannequin, then folds it carefully over one arm.

VOICE: He just sent a letter to this bleached blonde bombshell he knows in Winnipeg. But first he painted his lips with lipstick which he borrowed from some local bombshell, and he put a big red kiss on the envelope.

CATHERINE slowly loosens the knot in the tie, without taking it off the mannequin's neck. She undoes the collar button of the shirt.

VOICE: Just like Irene Dunne in that stupid movie we saw. Remember?

CATHERINE moves closer to the mannequin, not taking her eyes off it.

VOICE: I guess that's really "one for the books," as they say. *Pause.* I love you, honey. I miss you and I miss our baby. *Pause.* I even miss the snow. *Pause.* I love you, honey.

Very slowly CATHERINE puts one arm around the shoulders of the mannequin. Her head droops.

The "Beer Barrel Polka" fades up slowly, in the background. A male chorus sings along, not quite in time.

VOICE: And you have one hell of a Christmas if I can't write again before then.

Pause. CATHERINE does not move. The polka continues into the next scene.

TALONBOOKS—PLAYS IN PRINT 1980

Aléola—Gaëtan Charlebois
After Abraham—Ron Chudley
Sainte-Marie Among the Hurons—James W. Nichol
The Lionel Touch—George Hulme
Balconville—David Fennario
Maggie & Pierre—Linda Griffiths
Waiting for the Parade—John Murrell
The Twilight Dinner & Other Plays—Lennox Brown

TALONBOOKS—THEATRE FOR THE YOUNG

Raft Baby—Dennis Foon
The Windigo—Dennis Foon
Heracles—Dennis Foon
A Chain of Words—Irene N. Watts
Apple Butter—James Reaney
Geography Match—James Reaney
Names and Nicknames—James Reaney
Ignoramus—James Reaney
A Teacher's Guide to Theatre for Young People—Jane Howard Baker
A Mirror of Our Dreams—Joyce Doolittle and Zina Barnieh